Monkey Boys

by Alistair Gentry

alistair gentry

First published London, 1999 by Spacehopper
(Spacehopper is an imprint and trading name of Pulp Faction Ltd)
e-mail spacehopper@pulpfact.demon.co.uk
Spacehopper, PO Box 12171, London N19 3HB

©1999 Alistair Gentry
'Monkey Boys' is a work of fiction,
any resemblance to real persons or events is coincidental.
ISBN 1901072 207

Author photograph Merrilees Brown
Cover design by BigCorporateDisco
Printed in England by Cox and Wyman

monkey boys

monkey boys

HE WAS NEVER WHETHER he stepped out into the road or just stumbled. Walking and falling at the same time was a familiar state to him. His eyes were tired and he could afford to close them, because he knew what was coming. Let out one huge breath and worry later about taking another. For a few seconds he enjoyed floating in the perfect silence he had found. Then he burst against the tarmac like a carrier bag full of raw chicken. It hurt more than he had ever hurt before.

Nick lay shadowed by the bus, a lager yellow wedge against a cloudy sky whose colour he couldn't even be bothered to work out. There was an exclamation mark of ochre stuff on the windscreen, the kind of splash a huge insect might make when it met a moving vehicle. His blood. More of it came away on his hand when he touched his face.

He was distantly aware of somebody undoing his wet shirt. It hadn't been wet a minute ago. Being undressed was another everyday sensation to Nick, but where were those efficient hands coming from?

An elegant fifty foot woman with relaxed hair stood over him, her briefcase hugged against her chest. Didn't touch him.

'Shit,' she said quietly. 'Shit. Shit. Shit.'

alistair gentry

It was so shit that she left before the ambulance came.
Yeah, Nick wanted to say. It's a shit life.

A wiry version of Nick was reflected in the window of the duty nurse's counter, rendered haggard and slightly bug-eyed by a rough decade. Not much to look at except the teeth so very slightly crooked only Nick knew they were, the persistent stubble, the spirit-damaged eyes, the problem hair he'd solved by having most of it cut off. Now he had black Action Man fuzz. Everybody joked that Nick looked like a corpse. He did look breakable, almost see-through, but his face was as mercurial and expressive as a cartoon character's. He still had all the direction and grace of a 747 with one wing. Nick was still Nick.

He was nervously jiggling his right leg up and down, a body language rant about not being allowed to smoke. Nick tried to distract himself by using the glass to look surreptitiously at the man beside him. He had two sticks, one white, one aluminium, propped between his legs, and kept holding old magazines up to his face in a reading pose. Occasionally they were upside-down but he didn't notice or didn't care. When the old man lowered his

monkey boys

magazine, Nick couldn't help noticing how his eyeballs kept rolling up into his head. They were far more interested in what was going on inside there than in anything the outside world had to offer. The nurse called out a name, and it only took Nick about a minute to work out that it was his.

When he limped out of the hospital, his hands were shaking. A fatigued-looking man stood to one side of the entrance, half concealed by a sign, smoking vehemently.

'Can I pinch one from you?' asked Nick.

The man silently offered him the packet with the beleaguered camaraderie of a career smoker. He lit Nick's, finished his own and immediately withdrew another. Nick inhaled his first drag with due reverence, then turned to his companion.

'Have you been told off yet?'

The smoker wrinkled up his nose and shook his head. 'I don't think they'd dare,' he said, using his heel to pulverise the previous dog-end once more.

'I just take it for granted that even in the places I'm allowed to smoke, I'll be disapproved of,' Nick said, jabbing a thumb at the SRN who was giving him plenty of smoking room.

The man chuckled bitterly, but didn't break his rhythm of

alistair gentry

puff and exhale.

'I've got lung cancer anyway. Nothing much else to lose after that, is there?'

Nothing to say, either. Nick got the bus home and this time he managed to keep himself from falling underneath it. As the streets unwound themselves he remembered laying on his front as his legs were bent for him, posed like a doll. There was little distraction other than the skeleton diagram on the osteopath's wall. He knew it almost by heart now. The frustration bone is connected to the smoking bone. The smoking bone is connected to the drinking bone. And the drinking bone is connected to the I shouldn't have had sex with that person bone. That bone is connected to the I should have dealt with these issues with my parents when I had the chance bone, which is connected to the so I'm taking it out on myself bone.

The shower curtain opaqued the rest of the room. Despite the fact that he hated having the osteopath's hands all over him, coming back home afterwards was worse. The bathroom was the part of the flat that felt least like home; that's why he went there. Getting clean was peripheral. He rested his forehead against the tiles.

monkey boys

Revisiting where the osteo had been a few hours earlier, Nick's fingers quickly found the new ridges and bumps that were now a part of him. The gap in his eyebrow, the Braille of his shoulder, the pins and bolts embedded in his leg and arm as if the bus had left bits of itself in him. Something to remember it by, a lesson to him written in bone. An immunisation.

When Nick thought of all the other medical hands that had been on him and in him he felt like a Russian peasant, resigned to a diet of potatoes lovingly grown in Chernobyled soil. Here is my home. This is where I will stay. I have been remixed forever, upgraded whether I want it or not and there's no going back. After a while the water felt furry as it crawled down his spine. Its warmth was a pervert's breath on his neck.

The jittery weeks bled away and disappeared down the plughole.

Nick lived in a flat whose walls were blue. He was definite about that. It said so on the paint can. He shared the place with three cats and a woman that he called Emi. Nick told everyone the building was Art Deco, although in reality it was more New Town Municipal. The flats were subsiding invisibly. The floors looked level, but if you put down anything round, the object would appear to roll away of its own accord. He once spent a whole day doing just that.

Another time Emi came home from work to find him eating cereal at 7PM.

'How come you're eating cereal at 7PM?' she asked.

'Because I'm lonely. But I hope you had a nice day.'

Emi's face, blank as Myra Hindley's social diary. Nick put the spoon in his mouth again and spoke through it.

'You know... I just felt like having some cereal.'

Now Emi was looking at him as if he'd uttered something absolutely vile and without precedent.

'I mean... *why?*'

Nick hunched his shoulders in defeat. That's the kind of person Emi was, the sort with a talent for making other people shrug.

They met at a party in the house of someone whom it turned out neither of them really knew well enough to be there. Nick's discomfort hung around him like the smoke from his endless fags. There was nobody worth talking to, and he was seriously considering going home again. As the resolution settled Nick spotted one person across the room who didn't look like too

monkey boys

much of an arsehole. She was leaning on a windowsill, looking right into his eyes as if she knew him and wanted him to rescue her from boredom. When he finally fought his way over there, it didn't take him very long to realise that Emi hadn't been smiling at him at all. She always kind of looked like she was smiling at somebody.

For a long time Emi and Nick were into being friends in a sexual tension sort of way. Eventually they developed a bond that wasn't really love. More like the one that forms between a draining board and the bottom of a dirty coffee mug after a month of neglect than love.

Nick's flatmate at the time was called Phillip, and he was tall enough to wear a constant apologetic demeanour. His parents were Senegalese and had been hoping for a girl so they could call her Elizabeth, after their favourite queen. Phillip and Emi overlapped for about a month. The flat assumed Japanese proportions. When Phillip wore his little oval glasses to watch the telly, Nick knew why African sculptures look the way they do. Nick never said anything because he didn't know whether or not this was a racist thought. Anyway, there wasn't much talking that needed to be done.

alistair gentry

Phillip had just finished his MSc in Health Sciences and was going 'back' to Senegal, although the closest he had ever previously been to Africa was Belgium on the P&O for duty free. The reason his parents had left Senegal in the Sixties was a) they could b) it bored them c) they had heard about ITV and you couldn't get it there. They advised Phillip not to bother going all the way to Africa. If he really thought that he didn't know enough black people, then they could certainly introduce him to a few.

An ex-Rabbi from Tyneside (who had converted to Catholicism and androgyny in a big way) occupied the flat below with his girlfriend. She was a self-employed, obsessive German Goth and seamstress. Not necessarily in that order. They had long and extremely literary arguments all week. And on the Sabbath they rested. There was considerable disagreement about whether it should be the Jewish one or the Christian.

Before them, it was four student PE teachers who mysteriously took all the doors off their hinges for a bare-as-you-dare party and never put them back on again. They in turn succeeded a widower who wrote angry letters to the local papers about students spreading venereal disease and threw his washing machine into the back yard, where it had remained ever since.

monkey boys

Nick had to find someone else to fill the room before his landlady did because, understandably, he didn't trust her judgement of character. Emi was lurking around virtually all the time. She was becoming frightened at herself because she was nearly thirty and still lived on her own. Emi moved in with Nick, more by default than decision.

The landlady herself, Mrs P, lived three doors down. Her ambition was to buy the intervening buildings and fill them with tenants who, like her, were either ebullient liars or really did have backgrounds that made entertaining anecdotes. Mrs P was also a dangerously unqualified part-time physiotherapist for a local amateur rugby team. All the certificates in the hall of her house appeared to be clumsy forgeries done on a home computer. Nick was too scared to tell her that he regularly went to the hospital.

While Emi was at work, Nick surfed the interface between filling his time and pissing it up the wall. He tried painting, but in the end he decided that self-portraits inspired by survival of a bus accident felt as if he was sailing dangerously close to the hobby of a pathetic invalid.

alistair gentry

His interest ran out before his acrylics did.

'The colours are all wrong, anyway,' said Emi.

'They might be to *you*,' replied Nick, flamboyantly hurt.

Obviously he watched a lot of telly. There always seemed to be cartoons on; in the afternoon when he wanted to do something infinitesimally more constructive than doze, or at night when he couldn't sleep even if he wanted to. He cried his eyes out every time he watched *Watership Down*. *Akira* gave him ideas for his own private apocalypse. Possibly it was vice versa.

He'd given up his car a long time before, (too much for him to remember and there was that little episode with the drink driving) so Nick thought he would learn how to ride a moped because he could do that with a provisional licence. It ate up some of his time. He ended up hardly using the thing because all his friends worked and he couldn't think of anywhere to go. So instead of a method of transport it became a verb, past tense. Moped.

He decided to go back to lab work. As a guinea pig. He was still full of pins and bolts and painkillers from falling under the bus, but if he forgot to mention it to the company they might not find out until it was too late. He suffered from anomalous trichromatism. He was a chain smoker and was usually pissed

monkey boys

before the end of Richard and Judy, but he'd already got into over twenty studies anyway. Lies appeared in Nick's mouth as automatically as lit cigarettes. Whoring out his guts for a living is what he called it. It was a way to take the idea of being bought and throw it back in their faces, though. Or something to that effect.

'I am Nick,' he told one of the cats, 'I am Nick and I have my beliefs and I do not need to be justified.'

The cat went on licking its arse.

It was an unrealistic way to live his life and Nick knew it, but he liked being unrealistic. Nick thought his life might eventually make a great book. Not exactly an autobiography, because even he didn't delude himself that anyone would find the unvarnished truth about his life particularly interesting. Nonetheless, Nick thought he had at least one novel in him, and that he would be able to write it before he was forty. He liked to think that instead of just firing off at random there might be some trajectory to his life, if only when he was looking back on it; something worth writing in a book; that there would be some weft of significance to hold onto when biology finally yanked a loose thread on the jumper of his life and it began to unknit itself.

alistair gentry

STEREO MIKE WASN'T JUST a space cadet. He had his own geostationary orbit.

Mike had done far too many studies, and it showed. A short, intense, grey ponytailed head the shape of a rugby ball. Wide eyes, verging on black, that constantly darted and swivelled like a cat hunting in the dark. Time had worked on his exterior, and chemicals had conspired within, to condense him. Mike's skin was deeply ploughed, but so taut that the lines could have been drawn on in biro. His fake Fred Perry was usually done right up, but it was saggy as an octogenarian sunbather and hung in a loop in front of him. A ragged whitish line started below his left ear and ended just above his right collar bone. The piqué collars curled away from his healed wound like old plasters. He often felt people's eyes pursuing the scar. That was about the limit of Mike's dealings with self-consciousness.

He got himself admitted to the studies using a constantly mutating stream of aliases. When he wasn't in hospital or a research lab, Stereo Mike lived in a squat with a tank full of ugly

monkey boys

little lizards and a scrawny mongrel. It was hard to tell who the culprit was, but somebody always made the place smell like the changing rooms at the public baths with a top note of old piss. A man with a greasy centre parting and an aggressively wandering left eye would invariably show up, without being asked, to look after the animals whenever Mike so much as contemplated going away. Maybe it was Lazy Eye Man who peed on the living room carpet.

Their electricity had come from the lamp post right outside the squat for five years. Mike always wore his headphones, although he never had them plugged into anything visible to the uninformed eye. Framed by the silence of the street outside, tiny sounds became distorted and amplified. The dog lay half across Mike as it usually did, shifted in its dreams against Mike's heart. The night took on a strange processed tingle, fed by the pulse of too much current and the buzz of a substation across the road. Mike listened carefully. The reptiles rapped Morse against the glass. The town talked in code.

Next morning, the front bedroom smelled of dead cats. Bruce was a lounge lizard who chilled out forever in immodestly loose fitting

alistair gentry

pyjama trousers. He was one of the more permanent tenants at the squat. Now some of him had seeped pungently between its floorboards where he would probably stay until the house, too, collapsed.

Bruce was well known locally as an annoying retard. Sometimes he resembled David Lynch, but usually he was more like a picture of David Lynch as drawn by Dr Seuss. He was like your uncle or the uncle of somebody you know, only if he was making a nuisance of himself you could tell him to piss off without fear of familial repercussions.

Bruce's fugue (or his waking from it into real life) had started a few months before Stereo Mike met him. Bruce had apparently been on his way to a round of golf, but instead he ended up crushed between a Montego and a tanker full of syrup. He suffered concussion and a fractured skull. Bruce bore no identification, couldn't remember who he was any more and nobody came to take him home. All that was left in his new brain was a message deposited by God or someone speaking on God's behalf.

God spoke unto him, saying 'Lose the arm, Bruce. I'm serious.'

Bruce went straight back to the hospital and asked them to

monkey boys

amputate the offending limb. They politely refused. Eventually Bruce did it himself because he had lost his mind along with his history. He walked out of the squat, with the kind of purpose usually only in evidence when he was going to cash a giro, and bought an 11-inch circular saw at the local Do-It-All. Everybody there eyed him with suspicion even as he was paying for the hardware in question with the cash from his pawned golf clubs. It was no great loss; he didn't know the twelfth hole from his arsehole any more.

He went back to the flat where he began his holy assault upon the hand, which was by then trying to look innocent. There was little pain, no regret. God had given Bruce the answer before he had known that there was a question.

On that occasion Stereo Mike and Lazy Eye Man stopped Bruce doing any more damage. Mike knew all about the things they tried to make people do, sometimes just for their own amusement. By Mike's estimation between fifty and sixty enemies had hypnotised him in the past few years. They were always planting wild and foolish ideas in his head, causing brutal and sadistic oscillations of his character. Ant men carried away Mike's ideas as soon as he thought them. Buckingham Palace had him

alistair gentry

under twenty-four hour surveillance.

'We might be able to save the arm,' smiled the doctor, 'but I'm afraid the body will have to go!'

He gave Mike a dressing and an application form for an NHS prosthesis then sent them both away. So at the age of fifty-nine Bruce died of something or other, who cares what, friendless and handless, alone in a squatted Edwardian semi that now bore a blackish tide mark under the cheap carpet as evidence of how little a life means. Mike shook his head.

Why does this sort of thing always happen to me? Mike fished in his pocket for the magic doll head, gave it a comforting squeeze. It occurred to him that Bruce had been more than usually reclusive lately. Mike, too, often didn't speak for days. At least Bruce had good reason this time. The mongrel sniffed her way up the stairs, drawn by the same stench that had attracted Mike. She poked her muzzle around the door and narrowed her eyes.

'Microsoft can kiss my furry little arse if they think they're going to get away with this.'

Mike thought that just about said it all, and kept his silence.

monkey boys

FIVE YEARS IS A FUCK of a long time to work at McKing Burger. When Calvin celebrated that milestone, there was much talk among the employees that they might be granted three more days off a year. What did The Man give them instead? A name tag with the number of years they had served. Confirming that the place was a prison, an ordeal, something to be endured. The stars on their badges were millstones, not milestones. It was hard to say whether Calvin was paralysed with rage or just depressed to the point of immobility. When Calvin was meant to be taking people's orders he would simply stand there looking at them until someone else took over and pressed the appropriate buttons. Within a week he got the sack for his poor attitude. He disappointed the supervisor by taking his dismissal with the same equanimity as he had accepted orders for burgers.

Everybody needs an escape plan, and Calvin's was the gym. After five days he had bench pressed and Nautilised most of the anger away. He channelled the remainder of it into his newest obsession; being clean. It never took very long for one of Calvin's little fixations to develop into bloody great neuroses. First, he shaved his chest. After that, he decided he must shave around his arsehole. Even that was not enough. Calvin went on to give

alistair gentry

himself a porn star scrotum as well.

He would never be one of those clean-limbed super-adolescents who could model pants in his spare time, but he would do. Calvin resembled the halfway point between Jekyll and Hyde in the Fredric March version. Some attractive features, some primitive ones. Calvin's follicles were evidently overcompensating for their ignominious and premature failure on his head. But nobody could ever say he didn't keep his crapper clean.

Calvin hated being on the dole. That was the only possible reason he could discover within himself for staying at McKing Burger so long; the alternative seemed even more humiliating. He still hated being on the dole, though, having bugger all money and being treated like he was supposed to be grateful. He was prodigiously, breathtakingly ungrateful. For a few months he was able to distract himself between giros.

'I can watch MTV whenever I like,' he told people, 'I can watch MTV whenever I like,' over and over and over again. Calvin tried to use it like a hypnotic mantra. It didn't work. He had a suit but didn't apply for any jobs that might require him to wear one.

There were a lot of race horses in the town, a lot of affluent horsey people, a lot of Arab money and a lot of horse drugs

monkey boys

floating around. They looked precisely like what they were, too, more like gobstoppers than pills. The town was one big K hole.

Job Centre was a grandiose name for somebody's front room, and it offered three categories of employment: technician for the omnipresent Millennium Therapeutics International, help for an absent Middle Eastern gentleman, or horse. Calvin's knowledge of science was limited to reading the back of protein drink packets, his interest in other people's domestic arrangements was practically nil, and although he had the legs for sport, he couldn't honestly see himself running in the 3:30.

His life went lateral. Looking for jobs, not hearing from anyone, not wanting anything he applied for, and knowing he was probably better off on benefits anyway. He had one interview, as a night security guard at a stud farm. The equine woman at the desk wouldn't get off the telephone, just handed Calvin an application form without even looking at him.

'He keeps telling me to be happy with what I've got. *Be happy*. Well, that's exactly what I was about to say. When he says be happy, what he really means is be *quiet*...'

In the back office, the stud owner rose to the challenge of Calvin's bulk. He shook Calvin's hand as if he wanted to crush it or was getting ready to do a Judo throw.

'Well, Kevin, this is a very responsible position. You have to be alert all night,' he patronised, as if talking Playstation games to someone elderly and several slices short of a loaf. 'What we're looking for Kevin is somebody willing and able to keep their eyes peeled all night. Do you think you'd be able to handle that?'

Calvin waited for another Kevin which never arrived. The man leaned back and Calvin noted with disgust that he had his tie tucked into his trousers, emphasising the way his shirt bellied out. Meanwhile the horse pimp was examining Calvin frankly, like he would a prime stallion.

'I can do it and I want to,' announced Calvin, as he always did when he was bullshitting. The job was his if he wanted it. He and another jobseeking wretch were to patrol the stables. Motion sensors and CCTV had failed to even deter, let alone apprehend, the sickos who crept nocturnally into the stud to carve neat, surgical chunks from the horses.

All this was immaterial to Calvin. He didn't actively *not* want the job, even though it turned out that he really was better off on benefits. It was only meant to be temporary anyway. Third shift, split shift, shit shift. Graveyard shift, zombie shift. He had a lunch

monkey boys

break at 3AM. There was a shabby man who looked like a retarded Victorian stable boy who'd lost it to solvents. Calvin thought that even he would hang onto his job longer than this wreck. The guy appeared to shave about once a week, with a butter knife. He turned out to be some kind of supervisor. Some people can take it and some people can't. Calvin wasn't in any fit state to be counting days and nights, but very shortly he succumbed to the usual boredom and acrimony. One night he fed his uniform to an inquisitive horse and took himself home.

Life started moving forwards again and things got racy when Calvin's sister Leah showed up with her new boyfriend, Scooter. He was a twitchy grasshopper of a lad with the face of a child or a child molester, depending on how closely you observed him. Presumably his name came from the six Travellerish worms of orange felt on the top of his head. Calvin never saw Scooter take his glasses off, so he couldn't tell whether his eyes were painted onto them like his namesake's were.

Leah was looking thin as a vegetarian and her eyebrows now had a habit of restlessly hovering over her newly acquired specs.

alistair gentry

Calvin and Leah eased back into their old rituals. Calvin and Scooter could barely find a word to say to each other. Leah and Scooter had an agenda.

Going out for the night in a rural area really feels like going out because you have to make an effort. You can't just go somewhere. You don't hang out, which is just as well because then you might have to say things like 'hanging out'. You have to plan precisely where you are going, how long you will spend there, with whom you will go, and by what means of transport. You have to do it all in reverse to get home again, but it's even more aggravating then because you're inebriated and the buses are all privatised or, to use the technical term, fucking useless shit.

'It's like there's some kind of curfew after 7PM,' Calvin told them, 'Mustn't frighten the horses. They treat them horses better than they do people. I'm only worth thirty-five quid a week.'

Later Scooter and Leah bored Calvin shitless when they fell into talking shop, or rather slurring laboratory. Something about genetically manipulated crops and animal rights, two subjects that might as well have been labelled CALVIN'S BRAIN-OFF SWITCH. Idiot boyfriend perched next to Calvin with as much back to him as the snug would allow. Scooter's

monkey boys

body language consisted entirely of expletives but Calvin was too pissed to take issue.

Calvin got a peek inside Scooter's wallet when he bought a round for the three of them. There were two neat rows of brightly coloured rectangles in pouches, marsupial credit ready to hop out. Scooter noticed the expression on Calvin's face (where else would it be?), but all he did was raise one palm.

'We like credit cards,' Scooter said. 'We have several.'

It made Calvin green but he swallowed his tongue.

'Is that we like the Queen means we?' he said, almost masking his resentment.

'The monarchy should be abolished,' said Scooter, 'but that's another conversation. Me and Leah know these activists. There's this group, World 3K...'

World 3K had been digging up MTI's genetically engineered test crops for weeks, but they wanted more. They wanted to get inside the Millennium Therapeutics labs and mix things up a bit. Maybe get some pictures of the animals MTI tortured. They wanted to try and get work as human guinea pigs there, then deliberately screw up the tests, render them useless. The tests had been done on animals to start with, so they were already invalid and intrinsically without worth. There were also rumours in ecological magazines and web sites about patents being taken out on monkeys. World 3K apparently had no delusions about altering the system, or even changing Millennium's inhuman corporate mind, but they had decided that annoying companies like MTI was an amusing type of foreplay in a world where everyone would get fucked in the end.

The typical bastards ebbed and flowed behind them, drinking and pulling or at least trying to find that sensible woman or man who wanted to have sex with them, right now. Scooter and Leah had a one-sided debate with Calvin about what Millennium Therapeutics International stood for, about what they did there or World 3K's people claimed they did, tied themselves in Noam Chomsky knots, talked themselves hoarse and made Calvin choke on their endless rollups. He nodded along, bored, and wished he could be free of them so that he could get sharking like everyone else.

Eventually Calvin watched Leah's mouth without troubling himself to interpret its movements. At school she used to be that vaguely attractive, kind of strange girl at the back of a computer studies or French lesson who really was wearing a short skirt for

monkey boys

herself, not for boys (instead of just saying so). She was the one who always knew the answer to any question but would never volunteer it. She might even pretend not to know. The only pity was that she was his sister. Calvin pulled his own mental choke chain. Where did that come from?

It was hardly the time or the place, in the doorway of the Pap & Stile, while Scooter went off for a whizz. She did it anyway.

'Are you up for it?' Leah asked.

For a few seconds Calvin eyed her like a cat caught ripping rubbish sacks, without having a clue what they had been talking about. When it sunk in that she meant the MTI thing, he turned pointedly and walked straight into a wall. This didn't have the intended effect, which was to show her that he was not having any part of it. He hadn't even understood half of what they were talking about, but his brain was processing the information in its own fuzzy way.

Scooter rejoined them. As they walked home along a slippery verge, flirting with a muddy ditch, Scooter treated Calvin to a long and detailed rant.

'As if unregulated and unlabelled transgenic crops in our food wasn't bad enough, the fucking chemicals dumped into the sea by fucking multinationals are making everybody's willies shrink. Yeah, yours too…'

'OK,' muttered Calvin as the lecture went on unheeded, 'thanks for sharing.'

And grabbed Leah's arm as he skidded on the wet grass.

NICK FOUND OUT on a Thursday evening. If he hadn't been shivering and sick already he probably would have been more shaken than he was. He felt weird, disconcerted, disconnected. Affronted, although he couldn't begin to express why. He wanted to hide from Emi, lock himself in a cupboard with a bag over his head.

'If this is my best day then I really am fucked for life,' he told her. Then he said it again, for effect. He wasn't sure what he meant by it, but it sounded good, it sounded appropriate. Something he had made was inexorably contriving itself in the womb of the woman sleeping beside him. For the first time ever he began to imagine knife wielding midnight ramblers outside in the dark, trying the locks, creeping up the stairs to murder them

monkey boys

and prevent the child from coming into Nick's world.

At work, and when Nick was around, Emi could probably be described as a feminist. When she went back to see her parents, she patiently went through bridal magazines with her mother and never told Nick to get off his arse and do his share.

'I feel most like myself here, on the train,' she said, 'Between my parent's house and the flat. What do you think that says about me?'

Nick was somewhere between drunk and hungover so all he could manage was a brief glance up, to show that he had heard her.

'You know, Nick, a grunt is very rarely an acceptable response to an intelligent question.'

'Did I grunt?'

'Yes.'

'Was it an intelligent question?'

Nick hated trains nearly as much as he hated buses. He and Emi were trapped in one that was sitting in the arse end of nowhere, which wasn't doing much to change his mind. After half an hour there was an announcement that someone had fallen onto the rails at the next station. The wrong kind of person on the tracks.

At the other end of the carriage a man made sure everyone knew he had a mobile.

'Yeah, it's me. I'm gonna be late,' he bellowed, 'Nah, I think some cunt's killed hisself.'

Half a dozen people mouthed 'shut up' at him, hoping in their English way that vibes alone would bring quiet. Two hours, a free can of Tango and five overpriced generic whiskies later, the train started moving again. Public transport brought three words to Nick's mind: carless, friendless, escaping. Once he saw a building that could conceivably have been the research lab scrolling its tiny way along the snooker table horizon.

'Emi. That place over there looks exactly like Millennium Therapeutics. No, too late, you've missed it now.'

Emi had gone to sleep, her head against the window. Just for that he never told her that her hair had been in her mouth and she'd drooled copiously over the collar of her coat.

Emi had a younger brother called Jamie. He was in his final year of a degree in some obscure arm of biology whose name floated out of Nick's head as soon as Jamie had told it to him. Jamie

monkey boys

owned copies of *Das Kapital* and *The Communist Manifesto* that he had actually read, although he was actually about as Marxist as a Coke machine. Like most of Thatcher's teenage victims, Jamie was deeply ambivalent. Not about anything in particular. He could dredge up ambivalence about virtually any subject. He and Nick immediately got on.

Emi's mother, Amber, claimed that her hair had been white ever since a combine harvester killed both her parents when she was nine. The father put in an appearance and shook Nick's hand firmly, then disappeared into the garden all afternoon with a wind-up radio. Nick drank as few cups of tea as he thought polite.

'This is nice. From Waitrose. Lhasa Apso,' Amber announced.

At the time Nick didn't realise why Jamie started making choking noises and Emi nearly swallowed her tongue. Afterwards Emi explained that her mum probably meant Lapsang Souchong because Lhasa Apso is a breed of dog. Nick didn't see what was so funny about that. The stuff they drank was certainly brown and acrid, vaguely tealike, but it could just as easily have been radiator water or something Emi's dad used to feed the plants.

They had been expecting a real audition, but as it went Amber

alistair gentry

was primarily pleased to be in the company of someone who gave the appearance of listening to her unlikely ramblings. She clearly thought there was some kind of Romeo and Juliet thing going on with Nick and Emi. They both enjoyed pushing their roles as far as they could go and trying to make the other person corroborate some stupid lie that they had just told. Nick did have his limits, though. They made their excuses when Amber started talking about her LPs and indicated that she was about to wop out the Prokofiev. Spending a week with them. Jesus Christ.

They often escaped with Jamie to a pub that was empty to the point of being frightening. Emi wasn't drinking 'for obvious reasons' that Nick would have liked explained to him, so she usually got lumbered with driving them in Jamie's baby blue Chevette. Despite the age and gender difference (she was six years older, and still is) Jamie and Emi came as a set and basically had shared access to the same brain. When they were children everyone referred to them as Jamemie. Jamemie knew the theme song to every psychedelic children's programme 1970-1990. This was sometimes funny for as long as five minutes at a time. Jamie started sentences that were finished by Emi. They completed Nick's as well if he took too long about

monkey boys

spitting them out.

Privately Nick thought of Jamie as 'The Sponge', not because he was absorbent, but because his reasoning consisted almost entirely of holes. Emi was useless at having arguments as well. She could hardly remember what she had for breakfast, let alone a slight or misdemeanour that occurred more than a week ago. In mitigation, Emi didn't have any malice in her. There weren't many people Nick could honestly say that about.

They worked out what their Porn Star names were, by adding the name of their favourite pet to their mother's maiden name. Nick's family never had any pets, so he used the name of their neighbour's cat and came up with Tabby Smart. To him it sounded more like an upper class 1920's lesbian, but the other two still laughed so it didn't bother him too much.

'Phillip's been gone nearly a year and I haven't heard a word from the bastard. He's not sent me a sodding thing,' Nick complained, apropos of nothing except inebriated self-pity, 'No crappy dolls in made-up Senegalese costume, no letter, no postcard, nothing.'

The only sign that Phillip had ever lived in the flat was a hideous metal dustbin commemorating the wedding of Charles

alistair gentry

and Di. Nick enjoyed using the happy couple's eyes and mouths to stub out his fags. Emi eventually hid it in a cupboard next to the toilet.

'They might not even have postcards in Senegal,' said Emi.

'No, you're right, they probably have to beat on drums, don't they?' replied Jamie. He held onto her while Nick wrote IMPERIALIST SCUM on her arm in permanent black marker.

Jamemie (of course) won the Porn Star game with the inexplicably pervy sounding Pepsi Staines. Their unique Porn Star selling point?

'Being gorgeous, cosmetically enhanced identical twins.'

Emi found Nick drunk in the park, dragged him back to her parent's house and made him drink the instant coffee her mother kept hidden behind the grinder. Jamie found Nick drunk in the park and helped him get further towards paralytic than even Nick thought possible. Nick fell down the stairs on two separate occasions, even though he was relatively sober and paying attention both times. He went like a stunt man, as if he had rubber bones.

Late one night Jamie and Nick defaced all of Emi's magazines (her own avenue of escape from prolonged exposure to Amber

monkey boys

and Bob). When they got bored with that they did the quizzes. Are You Bulimic? Are You A Chocoholic? Are You A Fashion Victim? Are You Insecure About Your Appearance? Does Your Man Really Love You? Will You End Up A Bitter Old Spinster With No Friends Who Sits Around The House Complaining About Everything And Obsessing About Characters From Daytime Soaps And Game Show Hosts? Jamie scrawled SMACKHEAD and WOMANDROID on the foreheads of supermodels. Nick wrote NASTY, NO NO NO and WARDROBE ERROR all over the fashion spreads.

There was a particularly thoughtless questionnaire called 'Are You Asking For It?' which told you what the chances were of being murdered, raped, robbed, stabbed, shot or beaten up, based upon your answers to a lot of extremely personal questions like 'You are not married and you steadily cohabit with one man, but you have dated on the sly in the last year. Score one point for every sexual partner other than the one with which you live'.

When Nick couldn't sleep in the strange single bed Emi's parents had provided, he would look at Emi asleep three feet away and secretly cast the film of his perpetually unwritten book. Although it attracted a few stars on the cusp of the C and B lists

alistair gentry

seeking a project with a certain amount of credibility between franchised sequels, the film still wasn't anywhere near as good as the book. They took some terrible liberties as well.

On the last day, an oppressively empty Sunday afternoon, Nick was stupidly hungover and they didn't make it halfway to the pub before they had to make a vomit stop. Everything Nick had eaten over the past week seemed to come out of him in one go. Afterwards he felt better in a weird, alcoholic way than he had for a long time.

They went a few more miles, but Nick went (so they said) green again. The three of them sat silently in a layby. The heater only worked when you moved the slider downwards, so they had very warm feet while their fingers were still cold enough to start feeling like somebody else's. Jamie hunched over and tried to stick his hands into the vent under the dashboard.

The sky pissed on them so hard that the view across the fields grew cataracts. There wasn't much to do except look at the rain itself. Emi used her finger to draw in the window condensation of the only door that was black instead of blue. She did a diagram of a stick-Nick yakking beside the road. Jamie wiped it away with the sleeve of his coat and gave Nick a sympathetic

monkey boys

look. Emi caught it as well, though Nick didn't think Jamie meant her to.

'Hey, that was a real man moment, wasn't it?' she said. 'There's a real man thing going on, isn't there?'

Before the words were even out of her mouth, Nick saw something sad creep across her face, like a shadow over an x-rayed lung.

CALVIN LIVED IN A BESMIRCHED and relentless land of desolate theme bars and Dial-a-Babes, living out an exemplar of swinging batchelorhood written and acted into life, retrofitted onto reality, by thousands of hours of shit telly and tons of topless TV presenter magazines.

To a stranger, it would probably look as if Calvin's life involved nothing more meaningful than going out and getting more and more hammered, until he finally crashed sometime the next day. To an outsider, it would look like there was nothing of permanent worth in this world beyond the heartless and hopeless search for the next high, the next pec hugging T-shirt, the next girl willing

alistair gentry

to spend a night on her back and then vacate the premises.

Nonetheless, when Calvin miraculously managed to persuade some woman to leave with him; when he didn't get punched; when he could get her phone number before the place closed or she left in the morning, and it wasn't a fake, or even worse the old mirror gag he had fallen for a few times, 770 5519; only then would he be something most people would recognise as happy. Not that he ever had any intention of calling these women or of giving them *his* number. Calvin actually hid the phone when he thought anybody was likely to come back to his place, which was most of the time. He was often right. It was an ego thing. Sometimes people told Calvin that he had an ego problem. Well, Calvin thought, perhaps I do have a gigantic ego. Possibly I am so in love with myself that it makes other people sick. Calvin thought ego got a bad press. If you called it self esteem everybody seemed to dig it. So put it this way: Calvin's 'self esteem' had always been massive.

Mornings after, Calvin would stare at himself in the mirrored walls of the gym, a hard eyed beef mountain, and thank a God he didn't believe in that at least he was directing his energy towards improving on what nature had lumbered him with. Not like the

monkey boys

people he went to school with and had never been away from the town. They had ended up shadow boys, signing on, smoking blow all day, emerging small eyed and croaky at night to scamper across surveillance footage, prickly monochrome blurs to whom car radios and videos couldn't help but attach themselves.

Calvin could never allow himself to be like them. He wasn't like Leah and Scooter, out to cause trouble. He just wanted more than life, unpersuaded, seemed prepared to hand over. Calvin had put more effort into himself than he could begin to calculate.

'When you invest,' he reasoned, 'You're meant to get something back, aren't you?'

'My name's Sarah,' said the girl underneath him, bewildered.

There was nothing wrong with renting or selling the body he had made for himself, a body Calvin knew was so awesome and ripped it would make any sane man weep with envy. Calvin was a human cash machine from which he could make repeated withdrawals. He could turn himself into a franchise.

alistair gentry

THERE WAS NOTHING MORE he could say about the other thing but Nick asked, told, demanded, ordered, pleaded with Emi not to take the tab she had been saving. She did it despite him. Perhaps to spite him. A reasonably responsible woman, a social worker, dropping acid before she goes and has an abortion. In the cab to the clinic she silently tolerated his presence, but she wouldn't let Nick help her out. At the precise moment Emi's hand touched the door plate, she turned on him with an expression that clearly communicated the truth. Though it bust his heart like a Thermos chucked from an upstairs window, he knew. Once you know the truth, you can't go back. You can't unknow. It was half of Nick in her womb. Nick that she wanted out of her.

He went halfway down the steps backwards, mesmerised by her inscrutable fury, and lurched back into the taxi. The driver's head swivelled towards Nick, body absolutely still in the seat, his eyes almost vibrating side-to-side with an inexpressible hatred. Beside Emi's loathing it was nothing, though. It was just a ticking off, a mild reproach. Nick noticed the rosary and the saint on the dashboard. He didn't know her name or her story, but he was fairly certain that she did not approve.

Their three bored cats sat outside on the windowsill and

monkey boys

watched Nick masturbate while he waited for Emi to come home. Nick had once seen the results of an abortion in a school textbook. He knew even then that it would be with him for life, as it was no doubt intended to be. The street was covered with shiny tarmac scars that people drove over without noticing. The traffic lights went from go into stop and back again. As Nick stood by the window and watched Subbuteo men play on a distant rectangle of luminous yellow, he couldn't imagine what Emi had seen as they hoovered it out of her.

So they found themselves back with each other. Nick quickly came to resent Emi's 24 hour demands. They were always crawling with unformed insults and accusations, like bacteria in the chicken she once tried to hospitalise him with. Her monophobia, with its powerful undertows of denunciation and disappointment. Her apparent conviction that the cats were just miniature people with tails and fur who didn't happen to speak English. The pointlessness of arguing with her. The fact that her voice rose so many octaves when they discussed contentious issues that Nick feared for the windows.

alistair gentry

Certain phrases were never in Nick's vocab book either, and that included many of the really important ones. So instead of responding he would pick up The Guardian or turn on the telly halfway through her Minnie Mouse tirades, hoping she would understand it as a message of some kind. If Emi even realised that it was a coded response, it was one she couldn't possibly decrypt. Once, Nick called her The Terminator. She didn't come home that night. He never found out where or with whom she'd stayed. Nick apologised for that one, at least, admitted it was no wonder she was strange and apathetic.

'I just want you to get over all the disappointment and hurt,' Nick reassured her. 'Or, you know, whatever.'

She pondered this at length, then gave her considered response.

'You're in the way of the telly.'

While his mouth was talking pop psychology Nick's mind was somewhere else, fantasising about jumping up and down on Emi—like a child on a bed—to punish her for turning into such a stranger. Though of course he would never really do it because she'd probably kick his arse in a scrap.

One afternoon Emi stood in the kitchen and watched the Geordie Jewish Catholic in his sarong, whacking golf balls up the

monkey boys

communal garden at things she couldn't see, but which she occasionally heard shatter like cheap china. Silence had fallen under the floorboards. The Gothic seamstress didn't seem to be around any more. Emi cried so hard that her face became bloated and misshapen. When she was at home she walked around from Big Breakfast till Newsnight with water trickling out of her eyeballs like a malfunctioning Tiny Tears, regardless of how she thought she was feeling. Nick tried to cheer her up by sitting across the table from her and doing a Tiny Tears voice.

'I'm sad and unhappy... I'm sad and unhappy.' The reference seemed to be lost on her. Nick thought that going back to where they had started would be a thrill, a laugh, a scream, but they couldn't ever go back. Not now, because what he was currently experiencing could only be described as a scream in the Edvard Munch sense.

Like all good people from the middle classes, Nick knew that every form of sexuality was in theory OK. Emi had never really thought about it before, but she agreed that one should try everything. They also established that getting tied down and walloped didn't appeal.

Instead Emi played the role of a local woman who made it big

alistair gentry

by becoming a life size scratch and sniff pinup in a pornographic magazine. Nick played an escaped remand prisoner who was too enigmatic to resist, too aggressive to ignore, but whom Emi guessed would probably slit her throat at a moment's notice for a fiver and a Tesco Clubcard. Emi came home from work one night with a carrier bag, and in it was a very short, tight black jersey dress in Nick's size. On the same night, Nick asked Emi to wear his football shirt while he screwed her from behind.

'Do you trust me?' he whispered.

'I wouldn't trust you to take my library books back,' said Emi.

Nick didn't really want Emi to forgive him whatever it was he had done, or not done. What he wanted was the unquestioned ease in the world that other people seemed to have. He could even see it in Emi sometimes, less often than he used to, though it was still there when she forgot herself. Nick was one of those people who can't acquiesce, no matter how hard they try, no matter how much they know they should. Instead they wreck their veins and put their brains through the shredder. It was spring and her skin was perfect. He looked at Emi in her sleep. Half hoping she would wake up and discover that she loved him.

It wasn't very far to Harwich, and from there to Amsterdam

monkey boys

and Europe. Emi hadn't realised it before, but the world was almost big enough to hide her.

After she was gone, the empty, lopsided flat and the nightmares and the blue walls and the bottles. One of the cats got killed. A taxi driver reversed over him. Nick didn't notice the cat was gone for three days. Then he found the bin liner and an apologetic note on the doorstep. He gave the remaining two cats away, after eliciting a promise from his friend to have them put down before she would consider sending them to a shelter. Nick was afraid that, like him, they might end up as part of some horrible pharmaceutical experiment.

There were rare days when it was as near to perfect as anything can realistically be. On those days Nick felt as if he was invulnerable despite himself. Some days it turned mutant, frightened him back into his bottle. His world slowly shrank to Barbie proportions. It depressed him even more that he could ever have been as co-dependent as Barbie, too. Waiting for Ken to come home, tell him who he should be. Prowling the hallway, hoovering the edges where fluff would have collected if he had given it the opportunity. Thousand yard stares out of the window at telephone wires quivering with conversations he wouldn't ever

alistair gentry

be a part of. Watering the plants instead of doing the washing up, not as well as. Planning to clean the oven out of sheer boredom but ending up sitting with his head in it instead, trying (and failing) to think himself into Plath territory, or yelling 'Sylvia, have you left the oven on again?' to the empty flat and laughing until he cried. He remembered that you couldn't kill yourself with gas any more, and felt stupid even though nobody had seen him. Reading the paper from cover to cover, including the adverts for computers he could never afford and jobs that he knew he would never bother to apply for.

Although he was doing a good job of preserving himself in alcohol, he wasn't the kind of alcoholic who wanted to remain anonymous. Nick had attempted to publicly drink himself to death so many times that everyone, including Nick, assumed it would never happen. There were a few friends that he hadn't managed to scare away. Sometimes they came round and picked him up off the floor, undressed him and put him to bed. Or dressed him and took him to casualty, depending on whether he was conscious enough to tell them not to.

monkey boys

Please answer the following questions as fully as you can. The information you provide will help to ensure that your participation in this study does not harm your health.
On a scale of 1-5, how would you describe your health?
1 Poor, 2 Barely Satisfactory, 3 Satisfactory, 4 Good, 5 Excellent
To Nick, 'Satisfactory' always sounded strangely as if he meant the opposite. On the other hand, he didn't want to appear overconfident in case they put his 'Excellent' health to the test. So he was a 4, a definite 4. He wondered if anyone ever revealed that they fancied themselves as a character from Dickens by claiming their health was 'Poor' or 'Barely Satisfactory'. How is your health, madam? I fear I must report that it is Barely Satisfactory at present. I am, upon my physician's recommendation, going to Torquay at the week's end to take the sea air.

Are you troubled by shortness of breath or wheeziness when hurrying on level ground or walking up a slight hill?
Only when smoking a cigarette at the same time. This had to be some kind of trick question. Who would admit to that sort of thing if they wanted to get paid work as a guinea pig?

alistair gentry

As a child did you have Asthma? Bronchitis?
(Yes/No/Don't Know)
No to the first. Nick didn't know what bronchitis was, or rather he did slightly but he was too frightened to look it up and make sure it actually was what he thought it was.

Do you frequently have eyestrain, ear trouble, sinusitis, catarrh, watery itchy eyes, backache or back strain, severe headaches, dermatitis, other skin complaint, repeated attacks of sneezing, colds, blocked nose, running nose, bronchitis, diarrhoea or sickness, dizziness or fainting spells, eczema, throat trouble?
Never simultaneously.

What animals do you have regular contact with outside work?
Nick assumed that glove puppets off the telly didn't count.

Please describe your smoking habits.
Preserving the bottom half of the cellophane and only taking it off when he had finished all the cigarettes. Putting the little gold ribbon part from a new pack in the ashtray, then watching it writhe like a worm under the tip of the first cigarette. Smelling

monkey boys

(other peoples') empty packets. Making little men from the bit of foil that said PULL. Imagining what a piece of cancer looked like.

Are you currently taking medication, prescribed or otherwise, for any medical condition including allergies?

He liked the 'otherwise' part. 'Yeah, I've got this terrible bronchitis at the moment. When it bothers me I usually smoke some crack, which perks me up no end.' Nick already knew that Millennium Therapeutics were real piss Nazis, regardless of the study. At random intervals the subjects had to urinate onto a little techno stick, like a lemur scent-marking but nowhere near as accurate. Presumably MTI wanted to screen out junkies and dopeheads to avoid potential kid/sweet shop themed disasters. Nick, with frightening ease, got hold of a substance called Urine Luck! ('No need to fear that test analysis! Simply add to a sample before analysis and a negative result on substance abuse screenings is guaranteed!') so he had nothing to worry about. The abuse continued unchecked and unseen.

Have you had or been treated for Migraine Epilepsy Psychiatric Illness Heart Disease Diabetes?

alistair gentry

He did feel sexy at the age of eleven and was told off by a teacher for sitting in assembly with his hand down his pants, but Nick didn't think it was a psychiatric illness. Nor was standing on your own in the corridor really a treatment for attempted public masturbation. Au contraire.

Tetanus: have you been inoculated against tetanus?
Tuberculosis: Have you had a tuberculin test?
Have you been vaccinated against tuberculosis?
The curse of Charles Dickens. Tiny Tim strikes again.

Obviously Nick didn't fill in the application form like this at all. He genuinely wanted to get back into a study. It might give him a chance to get some blood back into his alcohol stream.

THE OTHER SUBJECTS USUALLY CONCLUDED that he was a malingerer. Nicknames attached themselves to him like his dog's fleas. That was how he had come to be called Stereo Mike, the most persistent of his names.

monkey boys

'That's him over there,' whispered one of the researchers. The two of them thought Mike couldn't hear them. Mike had his secrets and his ways.

'Sorry, I missed the first part of what you were saying,' said the other.

'You know, the one who's a bit...' pulling a spastic face. 'Gavin calls him Free Board and Lodging.'

See? It's time to own up to it, baby. You've got a really bad habit.

Mike couldn't keep himself away. His blood was so lacking in oxygen that under certain lighting conditions his flesh looked like ripe Stilton. His respiratory system was totally frazzled. Walking up stairs he sounded like someone using an old set of bagpipes for sparring practice. The quality of his eyesight oscillated daily between Superman and Helen Keller. Chemicals had used up everything his body had to give, but they wouldn't let him die.

No. Not yet. We may need you.

Like when the doctors gave his mother those massive doses of morphine to kill the pain in her head. To kill her. She refused to die, though.

Mike was a congenital liar. One day it was:

alistair gentry

'I'm actually dying of cancer, don't tell anyone though, I don't want to be treated any different because I'm dying,' and the next day it would be:

'TB. Tuberculosis. Got it from laying in a sewer after those bastards mugged me.'

He even lied about things that weren't important, like what he had for dinner.

Sometimes he really did see things that were not human. Mike never told anybody about that, no matter how far from himself he drifted. He was sworn to secrecy, as his contact never tired of reminding him.

Careless talk costs lives. That's what we used to say during Phase One.

Mike also knew that he was only aware of them when he wasn't on drugs. Like now. He sat silently in his bed with eyes closed and knees folded. The wings of a fly were turning lazy eights above him. What he thought in his head was obviously what the fly was saying to him.

Yes, telepathic communication.

The fly was a Space Detective from an altruistic alien race. Mike was resigned to the fact that it might already be too late to save

monkey boys

the Earth, but he couldn't simply give up. These beings took the form of flies, spiders, lizards or dogs because they weren't interested in making a big entrance. Mike could understand that. They didn't stand out, because they didn't want to. They wouldn't be on the telly. The Space Detective had told Mike the truth about television on his previous visit. Mike thought that cartoon characters made much better role models than real people. Cartoon characters were much easier to love. At least he used to think so, until his extraterrestrial colleague clued him in to what the real story was with the television thing.

Mike looked at his watch, a scuffed black digital effort with half of its LCD leaking. Only the minutes were legible, the hours just a subtly shifting smudge of black. His shoes, too, were so old that by some strange fashion lag effect they had strayed back into sartorial favour again.

The Space Detective angrily burned himself against the light bulb, frustrated by Mike's wandering mind. Mike winched his eyes closed. Time was running out. The things the Space Detective said were very much like the dialogue from a cheap Sci-Fi novel or a Fifties flying saucer movie, but it all made a peculiar variety of sense. Mike remembered that he had to form the words in his

alistair gentry

brain, rather than trying to use his vocal cords.

I'm sorry. I'm only a human being. I'm stuck in the past sometimes. I do hear what you're saying. I am listening.

⁂

THE FIRST THING Nick noticed was that someone had sprayed 'World 3K' in yellow across the Millennium Therapeutics logo on the gates. The vandals had hurled bucketfuls of thick ochre paint across the road as well. There was an overalled team scrubbing fruitlessly at the concrete.

The second surprise was the new floors: lino chessboards in mustard yellow and battleship grey, all buffed and waxed to the point where their lustre took on a sinister aspect. They seemed to demand notice and comment; perhaps to divert your attention from other, more crucial things. All the fittings were stainless steel. Even the cleaners had yellow and grey uniforms. The cleaners had better clothes than Nick did. The building had a disorientating layout as well, somehow both rectilinear and convoluted. Every long windowless corridor and houseplant-infested corner looked exactly the same.

monkey boys

The canteen at Millennium Therapeutics International was in Portacabins because the revolting stink of something very dead permanently hung in the air of the real one. On sunny days being inside the Portacabins was like being the bread in a giant toaster. In the main complex some of the automatic door closers were stronger than the average human being. If the closers wanted a door shut the best thing you could do was get out of the damn way.

The annexe where Nick's study was to take place sat a considerable distance from the main building, itself marooned in acres of grass and fast growing quickset trees, in turn surrounded by fields that sloped smoothly away to the horizon, not bothering the eye with anything it could interpret as a landmark. Everyone who worked in the annexe called it Monkey Island because of what they kept in the basement. The main building was (with subtle disparagement, a slight curl of the upper lip) the H Block. Staff had nicknamed the ridiculously long glass corridor that connected the buildings The Rotastak, because walking down it made you feel like a hamster. Or it might have been because staff seemed to spend all day carrying rodents up and down it.

Gavin Moran was the man in charge of the study. He was a

alistair gentry

doctor or clinician or something, and he had an odd proprietorial (but not their boss) relationship with the test subjects. Gavin's nickname among his staff was either the inevitable 'Gavin Moron' or the more inventive 'Morang Utan', inspired by his canoeist shoulders and the orange pelt that sprouted from collar and cuffs. They also called him Dr Death. Nick preferred not to ask where that little term of endearment had sprung from.

All the men on Nick's study were given one-size-fits-nobody blue T-shirts, each with a number ironed onto the front. Nick's number was seven. Only Stereo Mike's rodent face and non-functional headgear were familiar.

There was another notable casualty, number nine. He earned the name Norman Bates for the way he had of appearing from nowhere to gaze at people, or at nothing. NB also took every opportunity to strip to his pants. There was never any way of knowing how long he'd been there, but turn around and there he was, one hand hauling fingers through the thick black hair of his chest and belly.

To Nick's left, number six was a starved-looking student nurse called Tjinder. On the right there was a body builder who had some trouble getting into his number eight. His name was also

monkey boys

Gavin or maybe Calvin, but initially talking to him was like pulling teeth. He seemed nervous in his stoic, testosterone-addled way so Nick left him to deal with it. In Nick's experience the studies were the kind of thing a person had to get through in their own way. Although conversation was sometimes welcome, spurious mateyness was usually counterproductive. Someone always ended up crossing one of the many invisible hetero lines.

There was another team with yellow T-shirts, testing something else in another part of the building. They were all female, most of them pregnant. Nick found it difficult to get the bulges of those numbered wombs out of his head.

Over the years Nick had gradually accumulated a flush of research horror stories from technicians and other experienced subjects. There was the one about the two people who for reasons best known to themselves tried handling a chemical reaction flask wearing ordinary latex gloves. One man ran a few feet with the flask stuck to his hand by the liquid rubber of his glove before he fell out of the second floor window that his colleague had thoughtfully opened to let out the poisonous gases. They found the first man under a tree scooping soil and dead leaves into his mouth to cool the acidic smoke in his throat. Fumes overcame the

alistair gentry

other and turned him a shade of green normally only seen on classroom walls. Both men survived, though their respiratory systems were totalled. The tree died. It was still there, a hunchbacked and twisted thing that thought it was in an amateur production of *Macbeth*.

There was the story about the virologist who managed to infect himself with a nasty little chunk of RNA whose symptoms were a cross between syphilis and Ebola. Luckily for Britain but unfortunately for the virologist, his girlfriend had left him the week before. Over the weekend he died in his bed, burst like an overinflated balloon and bled to death. That one came from Tjinder, a notorious bullshitter, and sounded like an urban myth to Nick. Still, so did parts of Nick's own life.

There was Betty the Cancer, originally a few bits of tissue sampled from a woman who donated her body to science in the 1950's. The woman was obviously long dead but scientists had preserved her traitorous cells in liquid nitrogen ever since, grown them in dishes and nurtured them into a transglobal malignancy that nobody had succeeded in killing yet. Rebellious cells that not only betrayed the body and survived, but prospered by their treachery as well.

monkey boys

There was the Latvian company who wanted to buy surplus experimental dogs for processing into canned dog food. They probably weren't aware of the English idiom that, with a perverse logic, they made literal in their business. MTI was actually considering it to the extent of working out what kind of profit they could make, given the unit price of a dog.

The dogs were raised (along with rodents, cats and the ubiquitous monkeys) in an outlying semi-subterranean complex. As if someone had foreseen cutting out the middle man, the complex also housed the incinerator. Calling it 'the crematorium' was sternly discouraged. Everyone did anyway, just like they universally referred to the Lower Animal Husbandry Unit as Mauschwitz or Doghau, and the genetically modified crop project as Frankenstein's garden.

Millennium pulled out of the Latvian deal when their people warned them of a potential PR disaster; the British will happily tolerate experiments on animals if they don't have to think about it too much. They find it hard to cope with the possibility that the winner at Crufts might owe her glossy coat and exuberant vigour to last year's incumbent. In the end the Latvians got their dogs from Portugal where they were running wild anyway.

alistair gentry

There was the refrigerated and airtight Plague Room somewhere in the H Block, where mum could go to Iceland and get any one of a thousand lethal diseases, some discovered accidentally, some very much on purpose.

The possibilities for bizarre and—ha ha ha, so ironically—untested drug cocktails were as endless as they were frightening. The company sniffed everybody's piss rigorously but (Urine Luck!) they rarely found anything. Every piece of data they could possibly find about their employees was stored and endlessly spun inside a computer somewhere in Europe.

Despite all this corparanoia, it was no mystery where most of the quality pills beloved of local dealers came from. Although they were nothing of the sort, they were sold as Ecstasy along with the usual speed+LSD combo, caffeine, ketamine, the ubiquitous horse tranquillisers, antihistamines and dog wormers.

References to Aldous Huxley were mandatory, especially after you had seen the thousands of brains floating in a darkened room beneath Monkey Island. Most of them were disturbingly big and had wires and tubes coming out of them. Nick never went to that room again, although he did look for it and couldn't find his way back. He was certain he shouldn't have been there in the first

monkey boys

place, and frankly hoped that he might have imagined it.

Stereo Mike was quite a good source of material, too. On the second day Nick found him in the bathroom, which didn't have any toilets. The toilets were next to the dormitory, locked and permanently manned by some unfortunate in goggles, with a rubber coat and a supply of large containers. As usual, Mike was wearing his headphones. Nick carefully closed the door. He moved around the corner and Mike looked into his reflected eyes. Mike dropped the hypodermic. The needle snapped against the tiles. Mike dithered, unsure whether he should go after the hypo. The broken needle was virtually invisible. Nick kicked it under the sink and had the crafty booze-up he'd been dying for.

Nick never thought it necessary to ask Stereo Mike what he was injecting or withdrawing or why. Nonetheless, there was a pact between them. They knew they would both be ex-subjects if anyone knew, even assuming that the test wasn't already screwed beyond any hope of salvage. He was still particularly careful when the Morang Utan was around. Nick didn't know why it struck him as strange to find out that he was not the only one who was faking it.

Test subjects were generally allowed to wander around as long

alistair gentry

as they kept to their schedule, but the technicians tried to keep them away from the monkey laboratories. You could smell the shitty stink as soon as you opened certain doors. Many of the animals screamed constantly whether they had been used in tests or not. On the first day Gavin told Nick that all of them would end up on Death Row at Mauschwitz, even the control group. Or worse, their brains taken out and kept alive in that horrible Sci-Fi harvesting room. What Nick had seen of the rodent labs didn't strike him as too bad, if only by comparison.

The study itself involved a drug (for the purposes of this contract hereinafter referred to as 'the product') designed to make mental patients more passive and compliant so that they would cooperate in whatever other treatment their doctors said they should have, no matter how cruel or unpleasant. As Nick had suspected, the product proved to be a derivative of whatever it was MTI were furtively extracting from those palpitating, tube-riddled monkey brains.

MTI had spent years and millions tinkering with the monkeys so they would mass produce the product's chemical precursors. Then they tested on other animals for short and long term toxicity, allergenicity, mutagenicity, absorption, reproductive

monkey boys

toxicity, carcinogenicity and marketability. Did their LD-50s, saw how massive they could make the doses without them becoming lethal. Rabbits pronounced it eye-wateringly tasty. Beagles were happy to stand up (if only they could) and be counted among its advocates. Guinea pigs, rats, mice and hamsters had given it a tiny pink thumbs up. The ones who still had thumbs in roughly the right places and numbers did, anyway.

Now MTI had secured clearance to begin clinical trials with humans. Some of the subjects seemed to go out of their way to be awkward and demanding; whining about their schedules, telling the technicians where to put the needles, asking stupid questions, just squirming or not paying attention. Nick thought it was more prudent to be nice to people brandishing surgical instruments in his personal space, particularly after he had seen how rough the technicians were with the animals. Sometimes they punched monkeys a fraction of their size when they refused to cooperate.

The days went by and some people got letters, if they'd had the foresight to ask someone outside to send them. Nobody was allowed to leave while under the influence of the product, although clearly this wasn't out of concern for anyone's health. MTI was more concerned about its patents than its patients.

alistair gentry

Though the subjects had newspapers and magazines, their delivery once a day felt a bit Stalinist. Nick wouldn't have been surprised to find half the articles snipped out before anyone got to them. He mainly used the impressive selection of glossies to practise differentiating green from yellow from red, hoping he'd be able to blame the product for his capricious colour sense.

Nick was one of the veterans who arranged for little reminders like post. It wasn't that many subjects cared too much about people outside; MTI was like a Foreign Legion for the idle. It was more an attempt to keep themselves real. Mrs P posted on an entirely pleasant note from Phillip, who had mysteriously slid north from Senegal and informed Nick that he was now one of Gran Canaria's leading abortionists. Phillip stated this in the matter-of-fact tone you would expect if somebody were telling you that they were in Luton, had recently met a really fantastic woman and got a temporary job in telesales. Nick set fire to the letter. He threw it out of a window, then watched the paper curl up and shrink as it blew away to lose itself among the cadmium and saffron of summer trees.

monkey boys

THE RESEARCH CENTRE was a flat pack that had unfolded itself from a parallel dimension's branch of Ikea. Unfortunately, it seemed to have forgotten to populate its corridors and labs and most of the time it looked as though it had undergone a hurried evacuation. Calvin wasn't used to silence; he was more accustomed to making his own approximation of it by tuning out extraneous chatter and intrusive generic versions of popular hits.

As everyone arrived they were given a plastic bracelet with a barcode. The only way to get it off was to cut it. Bloated clipboards specified where they were supposed to be during every minute of the next week. There were things like '19:35-19:45 Urine sample' and detailed listings of what they would be eating on Friday at 13:15. A man with ginger hair and a good broad neck reiterated the stiff printed warnings on every page:

'... If you do not follow your schedule precisely as it is laid out, down to the minute, the company reserves the right to dock your pay accordingly. Wear your numbered shirts at all times...'

Calvin's was much too tight and although he was worried that he looked a bit like a girl, or gay, it showed off his definition very well. Ginger Doctor said the T-shirts were so the staff didn't have

alistair gentry

to learn names, but Calvin was already drifting.

'...by signing it you have agreed not to divulge or make available any information regarding Millennium Therapeutics International's Research Volunteer Studies or the product to any individual, nation, organisation, business, corporation, association, other group or entity not officially authorised to receive such information...'

Red Hair didn't sound bored, even though he must have done the speech hundreds of times. In fact he was giving it loads, like he'd got the best part in a school play and his parents were in the audience. Calvin turned to the man beside him, who was watching pregnant women file past the window.

'Man, this place is like a cult,' Calvin whispered. The man shrugged, expressionless.

If you're a fierce stone age tribesman, there comes a day when it's time to become a warrior, go out and kill animals with big claws, and do what men do. Calvin never had that kind of cultural precedent. Most people he knew had gone to university. Calvin didn't feel like he was missing out on very much. He didn't have anything to show for the time that had passed so painlessly, except for some birthday cards; but neither did some of them. He

monkey boys

worked at McKing Burger. One day he blinked and the majority of them were already more than halfway towards finishing their degrees. Afterwards they came back home to live in debt with their parents and sign on.

Calvin didn't know what he wanted to do with his life, so he decided to make it easy on himself and not really do anything. Stayed in the town where he grew up and found sex there instead. While not exactly free, it was cheaper than a student loan and could often be had for less than the equivalent of a week working at McKing Burger. Calvin had never really thought about it before, but for a while at least he felt like Alexander Fleming discovering penicillin in the ordinary mould that had been growing on his windowsill all the time. A girl whose way of showing heightened sexual interest was to eat her crisps faster and actually drink her half of cider instead of lapping at it. A girl who to look at really had the wacky sex kitten thing down, although wacky sex kittens don't usually confess to 'staring at the walls and ceiling a lot', like she did. This disturbed Calvin slightly, but he didn't know why. A girl who told him that 'The biggest risk is kissing someone for the very first time. Asking can you kiss them is cheating.' She said stuff like that as predictably and

alistair gentry

regularly as waves hit a beach. She just couldn't help it, and Calvin could hardly understand what she was talking about most of the time.

Then of course there was the window shopping, checking out girls who weren't even on the same planet as him, let alone in his league. The real Robo-Babes, Replicants from the Sex Asteroid, girls he targeted despite or because of the fact that he could never, ever have them. They were the girls who had already been claimed or would be soon by somebody a lot more attractively apelike than Calvin.

There was a long standing rule that girl du jour and Calvin couldn't sleep in the same bed together at his parents' house. In the end he absolutely refused, even on the sly, to bring them home at any time of the day or night. Calvin thought that if he was old enough to leave school, get married and drive a car (into his wife while she was picking their kids up from the local primary, if he wanted), then surely he was old enough to lay on the same mattress as a girl.

Then one day it was as if he popped a gear. Calvin finished with a girl who was a lapsed vegetarian and who had liked The Stone Roses since before anyone else knew who they were and it all got

monkey boys

commercial, and who insisted on telling everybody so. He did it over the phone as well, from work, which was not allowed. When his shift was over he went home to his bed and spent a whole day there without eating as if he was clinically depressed or something, although he wasn't. Calvin was pupating, metamorphosing.

He started doing weights to make himself worthy of the girls he really wanted. Along the way Calvin started to feel as if he might have found his place in the world, and all but forgot the origin of his obsession. Between the mirrored walls of the gym, the question was not whether he was clever enough or attractive enough, but was he strong enough? By the time he had the confidence to tackle the Robo-Babes, he was so heavily muscled and pumped up most of them thought he was a freak. Still, he had his successes and his ill-informed pride. Being ripped was, in the shrewd words of Arnold Schwarzenegger, like coming all the time. Actually, Calvin thought it was more like the satisfying shiver he had after waiting a long time and then going for a piss. It was like having the horn without wanting to pull anyone. It was a feeling and it was not in his brain, not in his stomach. It was a spine and loins thing.

alistair gentry

A man about a week away from a decent goatee (Nurse? Should Calvin ask who the guy was before he let a stranger do whatever it was he was doing?) tied a rubber tourniquet above Calvin's right elbow.

'Open and close your hand.'

Calvin did as he was told.

'Fist. Relax. Fist. Relax.'

The word fist made Calvin think about masturbation. He looked at the nurse's reasonably well-defined arms as he flexed and released his own.

His initial reaction to the drug was something like: is that all there is?

'Good,' he announced to the room, like the smug bastard he was. 'I've got the placebo.'

After about an hour, two words popped up and refused to go away, persistent as one of his random public erections:

'Thank you,' he whispered, too quietly for anyone to hear.

Every hour he was supposed to assign a number between one and ten to his level of anxiety, then do the same for his current degree of sexual desire. Each hour's pair of numbers went onto a little graph, with one axis for anxiety and one for desire. Calvin

monkey boys

didn't exactly grasp what this was all about, but he thought about the money and went along with it anyway.

He never had much experience of drugs, unless you counted the vanadyl sulphate and creatine to increase the size of his muscles, the HMB to stimulate muscle growth, the chromium to metabolise fat, the diuretics to reduce water retention. Calvin hadn't realised before that taking drugs changed things forever. Body and brain and bank balance. Suddenly panic put a plastic bag over his head. What if there were weirdo side effects? What if he had flashbacks like an old soldier? He might go tonto, become a Satanist and kill himself in a Devil-rite because of what they were putting into him.

Calvin discovered that his dick was hard in his hand. Flash images of stuttering undress. He was glad this hadn't happened in the dormitory. All there was between the beds were screens. At home he normally threw his semen into the garden. It wasn't even his garden, but it made him feel slightly less guilty about wasting the protein. The fist continued to move, almost feeling like it belonged to someone else. Calvin liked that. He had nothing to worry about. He was King Kong. Fucking Kong. He was fitter than a North Korean women's hockey team. If his muscles got any tighter he would snap in half. Unobtrusively Calvin looked for something to put it in. How big would the container need to be? Would they know he had been wasting his spunk?

༺༻

IT WAS HOT AND THEY HAD NOTHING to do except sit. During lunch hour, ant gangs of MTI employees swarmed onto the H Block's flat roof or the immaculate golden lawns Nick had not previously seen anyone so much as walk on. It didn't seem prohibited in any formal way. It just never occurred to Nick that anyone would, and clearly he wasn't the only one. He found it unreasonably startling to see exactly how well populated the complex was. To view all of its little inhabitants simultaneously. He tried to guess what they could possibly all be needed for, and where most of these people hid themselves normally.

The technicians and lab stewards from Monkey Island or the H Block seemed to strive for a dishevelled pallor, usually accessorised with a fag and an untucked shirt (for the gentlemen) or white T crying out for stubborn stains (for the ladies). The men from Mauschwitz, and they were all men, had their own look.

monkey boys

Menacing Men because of what they did and what it said about their personalities. The dress sense of child molesters. They thought that shining a laser pointer onto the foreheads of people sitting on the grass below was rather funny. It was even more hilarious when a man's voice started panicking loudly about blindness. Either stuffing cardboard boxes full of rats into an oven all day did something to you, or you had to be pretty sick to take the job in the first place. The scientific oligarchy were the kings of the roof, with A-level grace and jackets that gave them the shoulders of competitive swimmers. Without the jackets it was a mystery what kept their arms on, because some of them didn't appear to have any real shoulders at all. Everyone else kept their distance from these mini Mengeles while they put in their appearance, loitered, then departed just as noticeably. It was quite an exhibition. It reminded Nick of a dog show.

Ever since making the mistake of telling her department store letter-bomb story to one of the blue test subjects, Christina (Yellow Number Five) had been known as ChristinIRA. Once the story got around, she was constantly subjected to people who hardly even knew her shouting things like (Belfast accent) 'Christina, there's a bomb under your bed'.

alistair gentry

'Why don't we do a bit of yoga?' she asked, by way of changing the subject. 'That'd relieve the boredom a bit, wouldn't it?'

Responses included:

Yellow Ten: 'It might for you. You've obviously never been pregnant.'

Monobrow: 'That's in the Kama Sutra, innit?'

Calvin: 'Is it aerobic or anaerobic?'

Tjinder: 'If you know about yoga, does that mean if someone told you to fuck yourself, you'd actually be able to do it?'

'I don't know what you mean.'

Despite Christina's deliberate failure to see the humour, it gave everyone an image to savour and they lapsed back into silence for a while.

Calvin reclined in the heat, not realising his elegance. Collecting cancers. Dark glasses made him look like a photogenic Hollywood enigma, the kind renowned for turning down commercial scripts. The only rays Nick caught were by accident, and that was how he liked it. A surreptitious fag now and then. As Calvin lay face up on the roof's asphalt hotplate, right next to Nick's box of shade, he seemed more relaxed than he had. They got talking and the conversation somehow fell into orbit around

monkey boys

their families. Somehow. Nothing mysterious about that.

'My mum was a, whatcha call it, a compulsive shopper. Doctor prescribes her something mainly just to get rid of her, but at least it stopped her being obsessed with shopping for a while. I mean she did get a bit better. Didn't have no arguments over QVC with my dad and Leah any more. She even started paying off her MasterCard. Then the doctor has to go and say she don't need the pills any more. Just in time for the January sales. She took off like a fucking guided missile for Thurrock Lakeside…'

Calvin faltered and stopped, forgetting what the point had been in him telling Nick the story. Nick only nodded sympathetically, but it confirmed his conclusion that nobody thinks their family is normal. Everyone is convinced that their family could make some psychologist's career. A self-help book, perhaps. Learning To Love Your Inner Psychopath Who Murders His Whole Family With A Hammer and Then Slits His Wrists To Pre-empt Retribution. Alternatively, they flatter themselves that their families would drive the psychologist into therapy as well.

'I've never actually had a same sex experience, but I read somewhere that everyone is basically bisexual,' Nick blurted. The dark glasses swung his way.

alistair gentry

It's the kind of thing that everyone has read some place, but doesn't remember where. Nick realised that he was probably thinking aloud without intending to. He had definitely crossed one of those hetero lines. What the hell did he mean by that? Why the hell was he even thinking it?

'I didn't mean to say that. I was thinking aloud. Sorry. I mean, I didn't mean to think that. Maybe it's a drug thing.'

'Report it, then,' Calvin said, tilting his head back, erasing tan lines.

'It's too hot to move,' Nick sighed, inching himself out of the sun again. 'And I can't now because my arm's in just the right place to get this cigarette to my mouth and away again without anyone spotting it.'

They did a conversational handbrake turn, and Nick started psychoanalysing himself instead.

'Fear of women, definitely,' he said. 'Probably a few subconscious fantasies of castration and annihilation as well…'

Calvin thought his dark glasses prevented Nick from noticing that he wasn't really paying attention any more. Nick didn't care, because it was unusual for Nick to speak for the sake of conversation, anyway. He talked to hear himself think.

monkey boys

It was one of those afternoons that let Nick dream he might have conquered the major swells. Pretend his days could all be smooth and glassy. Dry himself in the sun, then get behind the wheel for the next adventure. His life as a road movie, UK remix, without dramatic tension, without the three act structure, the road movie where his relationship didn't break down disastrously, where the journey didn't degenerate from an optimistic Odyssey into a grisly nightmare. A road movie with no mental hitchhikers, no jilted lovers in pursuit, no mystery suitcase, no barricade of police cars, no exchanges of gunfire.

Nick didn't burn, either. Even the ultraviolet radiation that punched through the atmosphere like a nail gun couldn't touch him.

Shadows and sunlight made their slow crawl across the roof, always perfectly tessellated. Tjinder, Ben, Monobrow, NB and the others unobtrusively drifted into other varieties of nothing, back to work or off to the urine station to do their samples. Either that, or they stayed sprawled like butterflies pinned by the sun and closed their eyes, giving time a chance to slither away unnoticed. Faint cries of '…bomb under your bed' now and then.

Nick shielded his eyes with his hand. Emaciated sycamores

alistair gentry

clustered around the perimeter of Millennium's domain like desperate refugees denied entry. Farther away, a dense ghetto of older trees had established itself in the only unfarmable hollow for miles. Everything else was agricultural savannah, bleak with GM, TM cereal. Two halves of it zipped together by a perfectly straight concrete road. In a distant field the sun caught wristwatches or glasses and flashed signals from people otherwise too small to see.

❦

SOMEBODY HAD SOWN a mental illness seed in him. Mike knew that. So he had to survive by fuzzying up the issues. He had to keep himself as sane and safe as he could by arranging his life in ways that protected him from too much exposure to other people's realities. Stereo Mike had been in and out of rehabilitation and custody like a self-medicating boomerang.

'What's this all about? Really?' an exasperated doctor once asked, 'Putting yourself in hospital all the time, or getting yourself into situations where people treat you as if you're ill. There is a name for it, but I want to know what you think the

monkey boys

problem is. I genuinely want to know.'

Mike, who wasn't called Mike at the time, listened to all this spool out like paper from a fax.

'It's not about anything,' he said, when the doctor appeared to have exhausted himself, 'Like people aren't about anything. Doctors always think that everything has to mean something else. Fucking Freud fucked everybody up and everyone loved him just because he wanted to fuck his mum.'

The biro wrote, and wrote, and wrote. Eventually it wrote Mike into the Psychiatric. Black Fen was built in the Sixties, an hour's drive from nowhere and like most of its contemporaries was useless for all the things the architects designed it for. Not only that, but perversely it also seemed calculated to destroy its inhabitants either emotionally or physically. It could have been Monkey Island's evil twin. Or just its twin.

In both buildings people took advantage of misshapen rooms, anonymous dogleg passageways and open-sided mezzanines to hide from the nurses or each other. The only difference was that in Black Fen the inmates also regularly used its inappropriate peculiarities to damage themselves or their antagonists: splitting open heads against the sharp, square corners of pillars; strangling

alistair gentry

themselves on untearable and blade-resistant nylon window cords; slashing wrists or throats with glass skylight slats. Which is precisely the kind of thing that got most of them into psychiatric care in the first place. Confining disturbed and violent people in a building where every architectural feature is a Cluedo envelope waiting to happen must have seemed a sensible proposition at one point.

Barry was a grim one, even by the standards of Black Fen. Mike followed him as if he was stalking a pop star. If he'd had a scrapbook, it would have been bursting. At first it was just little things, like sticking a plastic fork in somebody's eye. They were prepared to let Barry have that one on the house firstly because he was a new boy and secondly because the man on the receiving end was in Black Fen for abducting primary school children. He would take pictures of them, then post to their parents grotesque, hardcore photomontages of the children's heads pasted onto adult bodies in sexual poses. The kids all lived. The molester went blind.

Black Fen was even willing to give Barry another chance when a Rastafarian (brought to you by the letter I and the letter I) hanged himself. He'd hitherto been best known for wearing a

monkey boys

long paper tail to obliterate his footprints. Not leaving tracks made it impossible for the evil forces of Babylon to creep up behind him and tempt him into iniquity.

The trouble was, Barry kept pulling the tail off. Barry never had what anyone the better side of sanity would accept as a sense of humour—even a sick one—so it must have been out of pure spite. Or maybe he wanted to see what it looked like when the White Devil led a man away from the glory of Jah. Perhaps he was going to ambush whatever duppie haunted the unfortunate Rasta and stick a plastic fork in its eye. Everyone, including Barry, queued up to file past and look at the body before the nurses found out. As if the man's parched purple tongue and bloodshot joke eyes were the crown jewels.

They upgraded Barry to the Secure Unit (making the rest of Black Fen by definition unsecured), and that was where Stereo Mike and he gravitated towards each other. From the beginning it was hard to tell who was the planet, and who was the sun.

In the Seventies Mike had lived mostly in Brighton squats. He wasn't called Mike then, either. A trail of cashed giros and credit card fraud led in later years to Brixton, Bristol and Birmingham (he sometimes pondered the Qabbalistic significance of the letter

alistair gentry

B to his life; perhaps all these places were just reflections of each other). He used to belong to a group that flattered itself with the name UK Freedom Unit. UKFU essentially consisted of Stereo Mike plus a few other dope-addled fools who specialised in sending letter bombs to the governmental and corporate enemies of the global working class. They nearly got some money from their local Arts Board until the police told the nice lady in the performance arts department that UKFU's explosives were not conceptual.

At the time Mike believed that crack should be available on the NHS. He was also certain that alien forces were shattering his mind with invisible laser beams and that electromagnetic gadgets had been placed in his neck and thigh while he was sleeping, either by the aforementioned aliens or by other sinister agencies. He lived in a virtually perpetual state of flashback; his life was one continuous bad trip.

Although Mike's rhetoric was violent, it was never deemed coherent or provable enough to get him arrested. His eventual downfall involved ideologically motivated Jiffy bag recycling and an unexploded nail bomb that he was too wasted to put the detonator into. Underneath the sticker bearing the recipient's

monkey boys

name and address was Mike's own.

Stereo Mike had been a member of the Black Fen Allstars ever since he hospitalised twelve inmates by poisoning their food with lead shavings from exposed pipes and asbestos from between the walls. To be fair, though, he did eat the casserole à la idiot architect as well. Stereo Mike and Barry got on like a house they had set on fire. It was the only time that Mike ever possessed what an ordinary person might call a friend. One might even say that Barry was Mike's muse, if one can imagine a muse with a face like a tumour and the charm of a late night bus.

Initially encouraged by an ardently empowering writer-in-residence, Stereo Mike wrote stories that Barry later magnanimously titled Stories From The Black Fen. Writing himself into being, or trying to write other people out.

There was this man who had been a dealer. Whether it was in stocks and shares or pills and powders never became clear. Barry gave him such a mauling that he was not only at death's door; he was broken and punctured in enough places to fold him up and stuff him through death's letterbox. Barry said that the dealer had been whispering things in his ear while he slept and trying to 'change his brain'. Mike didn't have any reason, but he helped.

alistair gentry

Research. Material. Write what you know, that's what he had been told.

Six months later Stereo Mike, too, was laying on the floor of the Day Room in a lukewarm pool of aquarium water and blood with his tightly buttoned-up shirt collar about the only thing holding his head on. Guppies, not quite ready for the amphibious life, suffocated amongst the broken glass and gravel. Flipping like bacon in hot oil. Already, eager spectators had carelessly murdered some of the tiny fish underfoot.

The last thing Mike remembered was a low angle shot of Barry, wearing nothing but Mike's blood, disco dancing to a twelve inch mix only he could hear.

After dark Monkey Island became a place of strange tranquillity, its fluorescent lit silence ruined only by the occasional vitreous clatter of a technician in a lab down the corridor tidying and restocking chemical cupboards. The repetitive hum and clunk of a kid on a graduate placement abusing his access to the photocopier to duplicate whole books. The comfort drone of the air conditioning.

monkey boys

Though they had never seen the sun set or rise, the monkeys still made nights for themselves. They rested their voices for another day of howling; whispered and fumbled instead. Mike had a pretty good idea of what the prisoners were saying to each other.

It wasn't as if there weren't people around, but Mike was alone enough and it was quiet enough that once in a while he could close his eyes and hear the sound of nothing at all except himself and his memories. Of course, as soon as all the nurses went off he would get out of bed and wander around.

Mike participated in his first study without his knowledge or consent. In Black Fen during the Seventies, researchers fed certain patients radioactive breakfast cereal every morning for nine years. Then Mike did one voluntarily, which proved (unrepeatably) that a person's IQ sways 10 points day to day, depending on what they did the night before. Once he spent a week having colonoscopic examinations. They put this fibre optic cable up through his insides. It didn't hurt at all, even though he was acutely aware of the thing snaking around in his guts. They gave him drugs in an IV. There was a video camera on the end of the probe so he could watch the whole thing. He got bored with it by the end of the week. If he'd known about it before, though, he would have had

alistair gentry

it done even if he didn't have a good reason.

Often the studies kicked off and Mike would think he was fine, but then it would all start warping and going wrong. This one was definitely psychoactive, a bit edgy, a bit trippy- but at least it wasn't too frightening.

Mike was still carrying around a Princess Diana doll's head, and it helped him a lot. He massaged the slightly yielding rubber in the palm of his hand. Princess Di had been stalking and harassing him for years. A few years previously he became so paranoid that he taped his curtains shut and enveloped himself in a place with no day, only degrees of night. He knew without looking that she would be sitting in her car, watching his windows like she always did.

Eventually he had to go out because he was on the point of starvation. Luckily, he met this guy at the bus station who once had a similar problem, only in his case it was Twiggy who used to cause all the hassle.

'That fuckin Twiggy. Too fuckin thin is what I say. Told her so. Bony little fuck. Yeah. Following me around.'

The Bus King had seven or eight doll heads attached to a string by their hair, along with a note from a dog's collar that said

monkey boys

'Please make sure I get home safely' above an illegible, rain-soaked address.

'Get your own fuckin head,' the Bus King advised, 'Get that stalkin bitch off your back. Lady fuckin Di, eh? Cunt. I call it voodoo. Fuck her.'

'I only like dolls when they're laying in rubbish,' Mike confided, assuming that the Bus King did too, 'Mainly when they've got no bodies and their eyes are broken, and half naked as well.'

'Yeah. So what? What the fuck? Fuckin...which half?'

'Either half.'

Mike was pretty certain he could blame this predilection on his parents for letting him have dolls to start with. Once his mother told him he was strange, then slapped him, immediately apologised and kissed his hair. He hadn't wanted her to die, only to leave him alone. They didn't have to try and murder her.

The Bus King had become engrossed in counting doll heads through his fingers. Mike assumed the conversation was over and walked away from the buses coughing up their diesel. The Bus King took a break from his rosary to impart one last piece of counsel:

'Fuck off then. Fuckin fucker.'

alistair gentry

When Mike was eight he wrapped his head in bandages and pretended he had been in a nuclear explosion. His brother made fun of him. A week later his brother threw his bike down the newly gravelled road and skinned half his face. Even as a child Mike had magic fingers. He would put his mark on people or perhaps put a spell on them, and something bad would always happen. He did it to himself as well, he wasn't prejudiced. Without wanting to, he became the master of Karmic injury.

The only thing Mike remembered about his father was that Mike always used to ask him questions, as most children do only more so. Sometimes his father would even consent to answer them. One night Mike had a dream he still recalled quite clearly.

'Daddy, there's animals.'

He woke and his father was there, looking reassuringly big as he sat on the end of the bed.

'There were animals. Animals were living in my skin,' said the child.

His dad always seemed to know what Mike was talking about immediately, and they identified the animals together.

'...Probably a marmoset, then. Half a zebra and half a donkey? It must have been an okapi...'

monkey boys

When he was very little, Mike often dreamt that the pillow he was sleeping on was trying to eat his head. When he woke up his mother would usually be shuffling off, his dad walking in, or maybe that was part of the dream as well. Then he had to go and grow up. It didn't take very long to reach the invisible cut off point beyond which honesty and expressions of love, even silent ones, were strictly verboten.

Is it Oedipal to know who your father is and still want to kill him? Mike wanted to kill his mother as well, but not really any more than he seriously wished his dad were dead; only in the sense that the young always think lorries full of the old should be driven over cliffs. The pill generation used hedonism as a disguise to scale the battlements of square commerce, then pushed the ladders away and bred inside. Tough shit, kids, we own everything and we're gonna live to be a hundred so don't think you're getting anything until you're far too old to appreciate it. The only thing that punks managed to DESTROY was their hair and they ended up Telegraph readers who disapprove of the Internet though most of them don't know what it is. People who thought the Internet was exciting realise that Global Democracy is brought to you in association with Microsoft and look what

alistair gentry

those laissez-faire pigs have made of the world, but what can you do? Anyone you admire lets you down in the end, disappoints you. You hate the old, then you become everything you once wanted to demolish, and it's despite yourself. You will be assimilated, resistance is futile.

So Mike's father, who once expected to be swinging with false-lashed dolly birds on a space station by 1999, who once thought he would be someone somewhere, worked at the power station until it had used up everything inside him like the alkali in an old battery. Mike couldn't help peeling away from him like the scab from a healed-up wound.

Mike didn't know how he had ended up on the lino. It was like a seizure without the sense of being seized, a blank flashback onto nothing. He noticed the intricate patterns in the hairs on his arm and had to stroke them.

You are becoming increasingly psycho, buzzed the Space Detective, with a slightly disapproving tone.

'Where are you? How long have you been watching me?'

Mike picked himself up and looked along the darkened dormitory to the clock, which didn't seem to be working properly. Men with pale, giant monkey heads (or were they enormous

monkey boys

monkeys with really midget human bodies?) lay under the scratchy hospital blankets and clean white sheets, like normal human beings. Sometimes their ears twitched in their sleep, as if they were having the same nightmare as Stereo Mike. That's what it most resembled, only it was much too real to be a nightmare. He wondered if he was the only one to realise that the test subjects all had such weird heads.

Mike had to find somebody who hadn't got themselves turned into one of the mutant monkey-human hybrids yet. Perhaps Mike had too, but he couldn't make himself concentrate. All he could think of was an old joke. Why did the chicken turn around and around in circles? I think it turned around. But why? Why did the chicken cross the road and turn around? But why would it do that? Why did the chicken turn around instead of doing something else?

Without warning, millions of tiny simian tongues wriggled over every inch of his skin like a salivating car wash. The monkeys had not stirred or moved at all. Mike's legs dumped him, shocked, on the end of a monkey's bed.

Mike watched the creature. After a few (minutes? seconds? hours?), and without any discernible provocation, the thing leapt out of its bed. It had what Mike thought was probably a distressed look on its oversized face. Insensate, inky eyes bulged out from either side of its head.

'You're freaking me out!' it screamed, eyes wide and all its teeth showing, a threat face, throwing down the paperback it had been reading. It scuttled away, sometimes on two legs like a man, sometimes forgetting itself and trying to run on all fours.

NICK WAS BOMBING. The colours were coming and they prickled his unusual retinas. He observed that the colours had vague shapes as well. Proteins, nucleic acids, steroid hormones acting like characters in private, hermetic, microscopic plays. They suddenly acquired voices. Quickly, infinitely slowly, they morphed into scary little kids wearing makeup and drag. Standing there, challenging him, posed there, a none shall pass kind of vibe. Just before he started to come back to himself and remember where he really was, Nick realised that the children weren't wearing girls' clothes at all. The kids were himself and his friends Johnny and Scott. None of them had aged since the Seventies. Their ugly casual wear and

monkey boys

malnourished appearance was surprisingly modish.

Minutes sulked past on the massive digital clocks mounted at each end of the elongated room as Nick's teeth ground against each other. Every part of his mouth tasted metallic, like an old 2p. Occasionally the other subjects twitched in whatever sporadic sleep they could grasp. Nick got through paperbacks at the rate of about two a day. It was either that or sit and stare at the bare wall or those infuriating clocks. His only consolation was imagining the money MTI paid him for his time running itself up on a gigantic imaginary taxi meter. Somebody a few beds away was listening to a Walkman. It sounded like boxes of spanners being emptied rhythmically onto a kitchen floor.

Nick eventually managed to distract himself with the book, although he had to keep reminding himself of its title by looking at the cover. He'd read so many novels in succession that they had fused into one blurred Möbius loop of fiction. Nick glanced up to refocus his eyes and saw Stereo Mike systematically, silently tiptoeing up to each subject and peering into their sleeping faces. Even Norman Bates had given himself up to sleep, although he had sloughed off blankets and pants in the battle. Judging by the look on Mike's face, he was enjoying himself immensely. As if he was playing some sort of parlour game with hideously complicated rules. A primary school board game rendered incomprehensible to everyone else by the loss of its instruction book and half the pieces.

Nick felt pity slosh into his head like the first drink of the day. Unlike Mike, he thought he had done alright by keeping his head down. Using his own mind and his own initiative because nobody else was going to do it for him. Not Emi. He didn't want to play games, usually not by anyone's rules, particularly when he didn't even know what they were. Nick never had the patience for Monopoly, let alone anything more complex.

And, worst of all, they were in someone else's workplace, being worked upon. They weren't one of the workers. They were medical appliances. You had to do something to get things straight in your head and live with the facts, or you'd drive yourself mad.

In the last few weeks they were together Emi had made such an art out of psychological torture that she could ruin Nick's entire day just by picking a particular object up, usually an item they had bought together, and showing it to him with a certain look on her face. Because she wanted to punish Nick for something.

monkey boys

He never really found out what for. Possibly it was for nothing; Nick was just reiterating his first impression of Emi, that she seemed to mean something but usually didn't. There was the crux: meaning. Conversations that ended up being more about what it sounded like to talk than content. She was aware of it, as acutely as Nick was. Both knowing that the person they were talking or laying with was only acting. Nick even started replacing the L and the Y that had gone astray from the end of her name so many years ago most people, including him, had forgotten that Emi was an abbreviation. As the days went by there was something about her, a certain quality only obvious with hindsight, that made Nick think of birds massing on telephone wires; ready to take flight at a tiny signal of which only they are aware. All this became normal for Nick, just as Stereo Mike's life probably seemed normal from the inside.

Mike was staring into Nick's face now, even though he must have realised that Nick was awake. He didn't think there was any point in saying anything, so he just waited for Mike to go away. Nick stared down at the two columns of type without reading, or even recognising words or narrative.

He didn't want to think of Emi all the time, or of what she had

alistair gentry

done. He tried not to. It was as if, without knowing it, Nick had promised Emi a piece of his brain forever. When he didn't live up to what he had made himself expect it would spill over into places it had no business being. He just couldn't keep it under control. He was too small to contain his own…what? Disappointment? Something far too slippery and cunning to be caught, named and classified by the likes of Nick.

Stereo Mike apparently intended to park himself at the end of Nick's bed all night. He certainly gave no indication of ever going away. Nick was aware of contemporary gender issues. He would never use the word cunt, but what do you say when somebody is actually being one?

Nick woke as if someone had pulled his emergency brake cable. He saw everything with horrifying clarity. He'd been around MTI long enough to know that rats or monkeys or dogs will use themselves up if you allow them to keep artificially exciting themselves. Give them what they want, give them drugs or electricity to the right part of the brain or even something as simple as sweets, and they'll kill themselves if you let them. Nick

monkey boys

also knew from experience that human beings were mad for stimulation as well. And why is experience always bitter?

Look at scrawny Stereo Mike, the whitest person alive, owner of a lunatic fringe cut with blunt nail scissors by a blind man with ninety per cent burns on his hands. On a downhill go-cart to death, suicide in daily doses. In Nick's head he was always dying, but not as fast as anybody else. The tears come easily when you think like that. It's easier to destroy yourself if you've got something distracting to watch while you wait.

Monkey Island was pretty much what Nick imagined the future to be like. A miniaturised world just big enough to support the bed of a lonely biological whore. Subjecting itself to probes and jabs, hives and jittery nights for the benefit of something so abstract it barely provided a hook to hang a metaphor on. It all seemed particularly futile because Nick had become convinced that although most people want to keep informed, when it comes down to it they don't actually want to know anything, so what's the point of finding out anything new? This might have been someone else's opinion that he was simply regurgitating, but he believed it.

Despite everything, the future continued to collect like dust in

alistair gentry

the corners and interstices of every home, every office, every street corner. In this useless place. There is a fine line between a groove and a rut, and Nick wasn't sure how or when he had ended up on the wrong side of it. At some point he managed to forget that tonight's TV programmes would eventually be repeats, but his life wouldn't.

At that moment the only thing he remembered clearly from the real world was the railway station. Nick's now had effaced almost everything else. The hardest part was standing on the platform for an hour with his bag, waiting to leave the lot of it behind for guinea pigging. As the town finally slid away like a bad film set and the sun tried its best to shine through dirty windows, Nick felt the pain subside in loops that followed the rhythm of the steel bars he rode on. Nonetheless, he had pain embedded in him too, and not just in one place like the bus scars on his leg or shoulder. More like the upshot of laying on top of a nail bomb (under your bed). It was as much a part of Nick as the colour of his colourblind eyes, even if he couldn't tell what that colour was.

The future was those defective eyes replaced with spare parts extracted with disposable plastic coffee stirrers from involuntary mental patients in Argentina. Nick was helping to half-Nelson

monkey boys

and Chinese-burn the future into that shape. An imminent world run by a gang of moron glove puppets who didn't even dare to admit their selfishness. Morally bankrupt, economically naive puppets. MTI liked to paint itself as bleeding edge biotech, striding like a giant Manga robot into the 21st to provide for the global free (nothing is free) market's chemical needs.

Nick's X-ray specs saw through them, deep into what lay where their shrivelled heart ought to be. They were a blind man with Parkinson's disease playing Kerplunk on a moving bus. Capitalist science on a long detour through the Dr Moreau aesthetic. A rubbery and fake-looking octopus groping its way into places it shouldn't go. Metaphors and metaphors and metaphors because it didn't really mean a thing. Millennium Therapeutics International was just a company, an entity that forgot it was only the outcome of a selfish ism.

Emi had told Nick about children using empty drug blister packs as pretend money. Five year olds catching cats and strangling them, just for something to do. Eight year olds who put breeze blocks on railway lines to try and kill passengers. Once Emi saw a boy wandering around in the street wearing piss-stained pyjama bottoms. His mum had written the word 'Idiot' on his head in marker and sent him out to meet her dealer.

'The middle classes don't really care about junkies or the poor,' Emi informed Nick one day. 'The only thing they truly, genuinely give the slightest shit about is the effect poverts and drug addicts have on the value of their houses, or about their videos and PCs being stolen.'

'Poverts?'

Nick wasn't sure whether the middle class generalisations she was talking about were in fact just him. On such occasions he simply arranged his features to denote attentiveness, as he did the afternoon they were stuck on the train together. If she wouldn't come out and say what she meant, then neither would he.

People like Emi seemed to deliberately inject chaos into their lives, with the predictable urgency of the unloved and unlovable junkies she pitied and feared so much. Nick didn't need that. He looked at it like this: never start sawing the branch that's supporting you. Unless you're hanging from it by the neck.

Wait a minute. Stereo Mike was still sitting at the end of Nick's bed, his headphones giving the motionless silhouette strange, bulbously robotic protuberances. It was freaking Nick out and he needed a drink.

monkey boys

'**A**NY CHANCE OF COMING BACK TO YOUR PLACE?' were the first words he remembered coming out of her mouth. The orifice continued to form other vague words through the lens of Calvin's surprise:

'…It's just my telly's fucked and the E episode of *Teletubbies* is on tomorrow.'

Calvin peered hopefully at Pubgirl over his pint of pissy lager.

'So what are you doing after this?' he asked. As simple as that. She didn't wallop him one or politely excuse herself and climb out of the toilet window.

'I told you. Looks like I'm going home with you, doesn't it?' she replied.

Pubgirl was an earnest but excruciatingly bad rural poet who liked to allow lonely, muscular men to pick her up in pubs. Sometimes she recorded herself having sex with them as well. Next generation bus drivers, inbred farm labourers, itinerant wannabe rapists, illegal container immigrants, fist-faced jobseekers. Her activities were immortalised in several home

alistair gentry

made videos with surprisingly high production values, which she proudly presented to Calvin for his birthday. She filed and alphabetised all his other tapes one afternoon when he was at work. They remained that way after she moved on.

Calvin had got it into his head that Nineties women really did dangle from office windows inspecting the pecs and abs of conveniently placed and unrealistically attractive shirtless builders.

'Women don't talk about men's arses or anything of the sort,' Pubgirl reassured him. 'No, actually if there are women who do, and there might be, then they've obviously seen too many ads or read stupid magazine articles and think it's kind of their feminine duty to talk about men's arses.'

Calvin remained, as always, transparently assured of his opinion and unconvinced by anyone else's.

'Look,' Pubgirl said, 'I only know what I want, or do I mean only I know what I want? Whatever. The trouble is I can't tell anybody what it is and I'm more or less convinced I'll never get it anyway.'

This must be great material, she thought. She looked around for a piece of paper and a pen to write down this blinding insight into herself.

monkey boys

Calvin flirted with Pubgirl without realising how good at it he was, or being conscious of his own awkwardness. As if Pubgirl had touched some emotional gag reflex point, everything came vomiting out of Calvin like a mouthful of puke. His mum's oblique references to Gay and Lesbian Switchboard every time he saw her. All the jumbled up almost-love and secret pity in him. All the stuff that was poisoning him.

Pubgirl's parents had a caravan in Norfolk, so she and Calvin rolled in that direction by way of a sort of month relationship anniversary thing.

Like all caravan parks, the place radiated a profound sense of despair when the weather was anything but perfect, and it was only ever perfect for one or two days a year. There was a miasma of disappointment over the place, beneath even the most meagre of hopes, mustard gas for the spirit. Put a theoretical Mahatma Gandhi and Dr Martin Luther King in a caravan for a week at the end of September and you'd better hide any cutlery that isn't plastic and lock up the Anadin. Calvin and Pubgirl were never going to be nominees for the Nobel Peace Prize, or even for a filmed insert on a heart-warming Saturday night prolefeed light entertainment show. The result of Pubgirl and Calvin's

alistair gentry

confinement was inevitable.

The caravan shifted slightly to one side as it braced itself against the wind blowing flinty across the North Sea. The coloured light bulbs that infest seaside towns jingled, necklaces of multiracial electric ticks. One day Calvin pushed Pubgirl's face against wood-effect Formica and left a greasy flesh-coloured crescent she wiped away with a J-Cloth and a sigh later on. Strange thumpings among the off-season white boxes. Duralex glasses doing more damage to the flimsy Fabloned walls than to the projectiles themselves or the person at whom they were thrown. The autumn sky razor flat. Pubgirl sat on a metal step with ridges that hurt her skinny arse and smoked Silkie after Silkie while Calvin tried to crash on a bed too narrow and flimsy for anyone but the most etiolated of smackhead supermodels to sleep comfortably in.

Despite all this, they stayed. The week they had planned at the caravan bloated into a hellish month and a half. A fortnight after they left, the caravan fell off a cliff into the sea, along with half the park itself. Had Calvin been more literate, he might have taken this as a metaphor.

monkey boys

Great abs,' noted Red Hair. 'Tight obliques.' Although Calvin didn't know the man, he recognised the voice of a fellow endorphin addict. Homophobic as he was, even Calvin knew that the man was not making advances. This was a free evaluation. The man spoke about Calvin's body like it was a possession, something he had brought along with him to the study. He was right. He addressed Calvin's muscles directly, rightly and respectfully, as if they had lives of their own and would continue to swell under the influence of such praise.

As the doctor turned around and stooped over a tray of syringes, Calvin noticed the lats pushing against the thin polycotton of his shirt. Calvin thought they were the most interesting line of a man's body, making muscled wings of the back. He could never see his own Latissimus Dorsi properly, not as other people did. Calvin was sure that his looked a lot more impressive than the doctor's. They had to. Calvin was a true gym monster. The doctor was obviously just a dabbler.

'You can get back into bed now,' the doctor said. Something in the way he expressed his authority seemed to turn what should have been benevolent suggestions into commands that Calvin had no choice but to obey. Calvin got back into bed. He was finding the 'experiments' increasingly obnoxious.

Suddenly Calvin was mugged by a hostility so enormous he was amazed he hadn't seen it lurking in the bushes.

'I'd hit you with my Kung Fu fist,' thought Calvin, 'but you'd only die.'

'Sorry?'

Why, what have you done? Calvin thought, and this time managed to keep the words inside his head, though they still tried to force their way out. What have you done? What have you done?

Apart from his mouth running away from him, Calvin felt totally straight. He rolled over onto his side to see what was going on.

Nick obviously had some kind of problem. No musculature to speak of. He was lolling around grinning at some non-existent joke. He kept asking the technician to massage his head.

After a few hours Calvin's jaws had got themselves knotted up like macramé from grinding his teeth. Trying to close his eyes or have a sleep brought on geometric Technicolour hallucinations, which superimposed themselves on his eyelids. Nick apparently didn't want his head massaged any more. He was now sitting upright and examining the wall with the googly eyes of a stuffed

monkey boys

toy. One of the other subjects couldn't seem to stop smiling maniacally as he walked up and down the dormitory.

The restless subject, number thirteen, the old man with the headphones that they called Stereo Mike, was suddenly watching Calvin intently with a weird look on his equally bizarre face. His inky eyes, though, were like God in the sky of his face and Calvin couldn't help staring into them while he waited for the oscillating fan to swing back his way. When it finally did return to him, a month later, Calvin managed to tear himself away from the casualty. He tried looking at the other people instead. It did nothing to divert him. None of them were moving and their totally expressionless faces only added to the boredom factor. Calvin rolled his head back the other way. The old man was in the process of disappearing through the dormitory door, trailing a monkey's tail of flex.

Calvin dressed himself in the dark. He was momentarily distracted by the feeling of his own chest, the underlying pectorals, skin like tissue paper, overlaid by the rough, rasping texture of shaved hair growing back. Eventually he managed to get his head through the right hole and each shoe more likely than not on the correct foot.

alistair gentry

THE LIBRARY AT MTI WAS NEVER LOCKED. Sometimes Mike went there at night, to sit in the humming dark. There were places to hide between the shelves where the cameras couldn't see. He felt safer in the library; surveillance abated there. The sheer bulk of the books muffled his radioactive burden of knowledge with their own. Although vaguely alphabetised by author, the collection otherwise formed a jumble of subject and genre, fiction and non-fiction. People regularly nicked the library books, replaced them with whatever they had brought with them to read, then took the stolen ones away when they went home. The original stock only remained when it was too tedious to half inch.

Mike never read books and hadn't picked up a newspaper in twenty years, but still he felt reassured by the rows of letters running from top to bottom: author, title, publisher, author, title, publisher. He gently ran his fingers over the perfect bound horizontal steps. Evenly spaced rectangular shadows, cast by protruding spines, reminded him of open graves for people hollowed out and elongated by some terrible virus. Mike abruptly

monkey boys

felt drained and lay down where he was, on his side between two stacks. On his back with shelves left and right, between B and D, looking at the ceiling. Most of the authors seemed to be French. After an acute illness he had rolled down into his grave. Graves, graves again.

Mike saw himself staggering towards his own end, walking in the last days. Knowing that with everyone gone and everything over, what remained of the human race had nothing left to hope for but the rapture that would kill him. Even when they were all dead, Millennium's monkey-brained cyborgs would rob the graves with JCBs and carry on with the program. The idea of his own extinction wrapped Mike up so tight that he couldn't move, but instead of suffocating and crushing him it was a comfort, a hug. Some part of him remembered that he would be coming down soon, that he would be cold and need to piss. But still the past and the product held onto Mike's feet like drowners.

CALVIN HAD ONLY BEEN SEEKING to relieve the boredom of insomnia, sheer nosiness really, but it seemed he had

alistair gentry

blundered into espionage.

The thought occurred that it might be none of his business. He considered this idea for about a second, until it was pharmaceutically removed. Calvin knew lack of sleep must be showing around his eyes. They probably looked like something you'd find stuck underneath a rock at low tide. There was an ache behind them, a tender sensation across his scalp.

Stereo Mike's furtive shadow crept methodically around the walls of the library. His face was a slow white smear, his body a bleached blur in search of something. He touched each spine in turn as if he could tell what they said in the dark. Either the test was messing with the bloke's head, or Stereo Mike was World 3K's man on the inside. Calvin should have realised earlier that the guy looked exactly like one of Leah and Scooter's mob. They couldn't exploit Calvin, so the bastards went behind his impressively muscular back. That was out of order. He never actually said no. Did he? Mike stopped to paw at the air, swished his arms to ward off invisible dwarves. Calvin thought it was best if he waited outside. The old guy had to come out eventually and no matter where he wanted to go, there was only one door. On a sleepless night every minute dilates into

monkey boys

a cliché of waiting. Calvin had time to hope his youth never oxidised into such wretched old age.

※

BACK IN HIS DISTANT PAST there had been a nurse whose unconditional care and attention Stereo Mike craved more specifically and more acutely than any other. He didn't know why, she didn't reciprocate; but even she ended up disillusioned with him. One day Mike disappeared with her car, her credit cards and about a ton in cash. He imagined her grave, too, as empty as her purse. Mike had to steal from her. If she hadn't financed his escape they would have sent him back to Black Fen, the threat that was always hovering where his eyes didn't go. Eventually, somehow, he found his way back to the old house. He hadn't known that he remembered where it was. He hadn't even recalled that he didn't remember.

Mike's mum sat in the same chair as when he last saw her, the chair where she'd read the same dog magazine an incalculable number of years before.

Until that moment he still half expected her to appear at the

alistair gentry

door brandishing a bloody steak hammer or a houseplant mister full of Paraquat. An award-winning performance in the role of psycho housewife from housing estate Hell, the part in which Mike's memory had cast her. Seeing her was like being hit on the head with a cricket bat. He had anticipated Norma Desmond, not Davros. His mother was old. Dr Cyclops had shrunk her.

Most people die of what experts, without the slightest irony, refer to as natural causes. To Mike, 'stroke' sounded like something that brushed past you, something that might give softly against the reassuring solidity of yourself. So how do intracerebral aneurysm and haemorrhage of the carotid artery grab you? The words came back to him like the titles of novels. Hemiparesis? Aphasia? When things got technical the language began to sound appropriately fierce. His blood vessels would grow tiny clots, the clots would blenderise with all the other poisonous crap that was swilling around inside him. Fouled veins and organs might someday get cancerous ideas; fat could throttle his heart; parts of his brain he didn't even know were there would decide to detonate themselves. Natural causes were, to Mike, the most disturbing ones. He couldn't reason with natural causes. His own body became a hostile thing that trapped him inside it.

monkey boys

His mother was in that familiar pose, fag in hand, only this time it was a jazz cigarette and the air smelled of blow as well as tobacco. She smoked with one side of her mouth, in constant imitation of someone exhaling away from the person they are talking to. On the opposite side of her head was the pink zip where the doctors had pulled to open her up. One eye zeroed in on Mike with the precision of a telescopic rifle sight, but the other followed at its own lazy pace. She stood to attention, found her balance. A few seconds later one hand pushed feebly against Mike's chest, the hand that had once been able to chuck a paperback with such force it could have brought down a bull elephant.

She couldn't even maintain this paltry amount of pressure. The hand fell away. She said nothing, though her mouth worked slightly as if she might be trying to formulate a sentence. Mike did not try to help her finish it. After that initial outbreak of hostility, he saw her for what she was. Lost. Heartbreakingly dumb, gone from him. Like Barry and his father, gone away to somewhere Mike could not follow even if he could prove that he genuinely wanted to.

Mum collapsed into the armchair again and stared at the wall. The telephone on the floor by her side had probably been thrown at the spot she was studying, and was clumsily but enthusiastically mummified with Sellotape. It was already going yellow and peeling away like old skin. The soles of her bare feet were almost black. A row of monozygotic china beagles sat in a militaristic line on top of the telly and observed Mike with heads cocked to the left and a cute glassy expression.

Mike went past her, and in the kitchen found what he had known he would. Sitting perfectly parallel to the edge of the kitchen table, innocent as a kid waiting to drop a brick onto a passing car. The manual typewriter, black paint chipped and abraded at every angle, the return arm snapped off halfway and keen, with HM BLACK FEN stencilled onto the back.

Mike sat on the opposite side of the table from the machine, half expecting it to start typing the story as he wanted it to be, saving him the bother of having to work it all out into some kind of order.

His mother twisted her head around to croak through the kitchen door.

'Barbara is the wrong name for something on the moon, isn't it?' she said, a sentence both muttered and urgent. Mike wondered if this important information was what she had been

monkey boys

attempting to impart earlier. All he could do was nod as if he understood what she meant.

The more agitated she got, the farther his mother strayed from coherence. Slipping into aphasia. A staccato history of nonsense in her fast junkie whisper voice. The deranged rantings of a lifelong drug Hoover. The story of Stereo Mike.

He was her secretary, writing, typing a fiction about Black Fen and the Secure Unit, the suicide of a Rastafarian, and about the dealer whose body just bounced up like a big crash dummy, as if it was on rubber bands or strings. Barry did that. Mike's left hand felt his scar from end to end while he wrote of the fish dying on the floor as nearly all his own life leaked out. Barry did that, too. The evening Mike found some mushrooms in a field near his father's power station, where later that night he met the aliens who had experimented on him so cruelly all his life and implanted electronic things inside his body. Barry took these objects out, carved them out, and Mike proudly fingered those scars too. Lifted up his ponytail to remember with his fingers the pink hyphen where his head joined his neck, and unzipped his trousers to palpate the longer S that made a parting in the hair of his inner thigh.

Barry's removal of the implants had been instrumental in their

alistair gentry

escape from Black Fen, although Mike couldn't quite remember how. He thought it was probably more important that he just spewed it all out. Somebody fell a hundred and fifty feet from the roof of Black Fen, although sometimes in his memory it was Barry, sometimes Mike himself, or occasionally one of their pursuers. Mike held on to the typewriter through it all, dragged it along with him, a literary ball and chain.

Barry and Stereo Mike stumbled all the way from the Psychiatric, across two counties on shattered stumps and beset by packs of dogs, to the house where Mike's mother sat between annoying visits from the community nurse and thought strokish thoughts she could never reconstruct the right words for.

Mike had spent his life trying to prove to himself that he wasn't chicken; but at some point he had started playing it instead. Running straight out into the road like a stupid Bambi. Life was doing a ton and fiddling with the radio, killing children and not its speed. Mike staring into the headlights of that oncoming lorry. He could see life dieselling over him and on down the road towards its destination, eating dual carriageway, leaving him behind as a ludicrously small red blur of fluff and gristle.

Mike never knew what the obvious thing to do was, except in

monkey boys

retrospect when clearly it was no good. All he knew was that having to think about safe sex was a drag, that the cheap thrills other people sneered at were usually the best ones and that although people thought that they were hominids and therefore better than a Rhesus monkey or a baboon, actually human beings were just as atavistic. The unfortunate thing was that having all this information at his disposal only made Mike more aware of what he didn't know, instead of more confident about what he actually did.

Through the kitchen window Mike could see that the end of the garden was littered with hundreds of smashed china beagles. There was some black amusement in the fact that these canine fragments lay close to where Barry lay buried like a dog.

Mike swivelled his gaze towards the typewriter again. QWERT YU I OPAS, it said. POI UYT REWQ. It talked just like his mother when she got annoyed.

A distant automatic door closer whined about its job. You are here. His mother's house was long gone, his mother stashed away, Barry interred beneath a bypass.

The body of the Space Detective was mashed against the library window. There was a diagonal smear of yellow insect juice where

alistair gentry

someone had killed him, then enjoyed the sensation of chitinous body between thumb and glass. Mike hadn't felt this tiny death as he should have. His alertness was slipping. The murderer might still be around, could even be watching. Mike remembered the Space Detective's last words to him. You are becoming increasingly psycho.

Looking beyond the murder on the glass, Mike saw a light in the woods. The trees arching over it, attempting to keep their secret, restlessly cupping it with their branches, luminosity twisting and knitting itself into the perfect agricultural darkness it had invaded. He didn't have any time to waste. He didn't have any choice. The Space Detective was dead, so responsibility for the mission must have passed to Mike. He worked the library window open. The landing site glowed among the trees. Stereo Mike set off for his rendezvous.

NICK'S TYPE WERE so commonplace that the staff almost grew complacent. There was always that one thing certain subjects couldn't or wouldn't leave behind. So the technicians

monkey boys

searched regularly for booze or cigs or chocolate or works or bags of crisps or whatever people thought they might need to get them through. Behind the toilet pedestals, or airtight plastic bags inside the cisterns. They checked under the mattresses and inside pillows. All of this failed to take into account the cunning of the bourgeois alcoholic. They never looked inside the air conditioning unit on the roof. That's where Nick stashed his second emergency bottle of Jack Daniels. The primary one was already dead. He'd been cheeky getting shot of that one, just peeled the label off and chucked the empty bottle into the recycling bin outside the canteen. The tertiary emergency bottle, full to the top of the label, was inside a disused storage heater in the library.

He was trying to ration himself. He wasn't sure how much of his nausea was the monkey drug and how much was cold turkey. His sensations, like his stomach, seemed muddied, refused to settle. He couldn't make the simplest of thoughts come into focus properly. Delerium Tremens, or was it just bloody cold out here?

Nick looked down at himself and realised he was barefoot and boxer shorted. Christ. He was starting to treat the place like his home. Next thing he knew, he would be answering the phones or

alistair gentry

going around switching off lights. Worse than that, he was turning into a Norman Bates or a Stereo Mike. Earlier on he'd had an unscheduled, unsupervised piss in the sink to avoid the irritating urine station. With the equivalent of a few double Jacks inside him Nick knew he would feel more human. He just needed enough to blunt his body's insistence a little bit, then he could go back to bed. His aim was to grab a few hours before they started jabbing and measuring him again.

He sat on the parapet and cracked the seal on the bottle, a ritual he enjoyed nearly as much as the drinking itself. The glass was polar from being inside the air conditioner and the ridges of its neck pressed gently in reassuring ways against Nick's palm as he tilted the bottle to swig. He actually preferred to drink it at room temperature, but the bottle's coldness combined with the warmth in his throat enveloped the night's chill almost instantaneously, like the closing of a fridge door. Alcohol was like that. It always knew exactly what he lacked, and gave it to him without equivocation or delay.

Being virtually naked was sort of turning him on, but he was confounded as to what his libido was directed at. Obviously to a large degree it was himself, his own body, its maleness, its bulk

monkey boys

and its bone and its hair. Other than that he was not thinking of any person in particular, or any person at all. The perfect solidity of the cast concrete wall under his arse invited Nick's own hardness. He wanted to take the air conditioning unit roughly from behind, give it something to hum about. The flat, subtle movement of the fields was sexy, inviting lascivious comments and a detailed grope. Should Nick lean forward and fall, by accident or decision, the unseen ground was waiting to fuck him to death.

The chain link illuminated itself as motion sensors stopped dozing. Stereo Mike had triggered them as he attempted to climb the outer fence, which was not an erotic image at all. The perimeter was rumoured to be electrified after dark, to stop the animal rights and genetic engineering activists from getting in. The experimental crops outside were regularly torn up in the night, so Nick was prepared to believe the activists might be out there. He was certain that Millennium would quite happily electrocute the poor bastards, too. Nick drank to their continued good health, although he'd drink to anyone or to himself if necessary. If the fence did have current running through it, even this wasn't enough to discourage Mike. He was going at it with minimal success, but the determination of a caged gerbil.

Since the cameras had apparently let Mike slip by unobserved, Nick supposed that the decent thing to do would be to go and get the old nutter back before he became a drain on the national grid or got his pay docked or something. Although if Nick was going out into the world he would need clothes. Unfortunately, getting clothes meant sending directions from his brain to move appropriate limbs in the correct sequence. If he was honest with himself, at the moment that might present a challenge.

❧

CALVIN SAW THE BONFIRE AMONG THE TREES before he was even halfway there. It took him a bit longer to make out the spidery torso weaving slowly away from him through the stalks. He yelled, but Stereo Mike ignored him or couldn't hear. Calvin pounded across the field, the ripening heads of the plants whipping and scratching at his bare arms. Eventually he caught Mike by the flex of his headphones and yanked. The cans whipped through the air and lost themselves.

Mike went a few more paces before it registered. His hands

monkey boys

fluttered up to his ears and he screamed. He screamed as Calvin had never imagined any human being could, let alone this reticent little man, a scream dredged up from some soiled, abysmal place where the profoundest of hurts could survive. Mike still had his back to Calvin, and the howl swooped like a hungry crow across the fields. Stereo Mike drew breath. And screamed. Screamed. Screamed.

Calvin scrambled into the wiry stems to retrieve Mike's headphones. Hastily he jammed them back over Mike's head. Calvin held him firmly by the shoulders and peered into that wizened monkey face, hoping to reassure the old man, resisting a powerful urge to shake him. The screams ebbed into panicky gasps. He took Mike's scrawny hands, placed them over the ear pieces, held them there. Beyond Mike's shoulder Calvin could see people emerging from the trees, climbing over or through a wire fence.

'What you doing to him?' demanded a bald headed boy with the contents of his gran's sewing box stuck in his face.

'Nothing.'

Calvin's voice was hoarse from lack of use. The immensity of Calvin and the fragility of Stereo Mike probably did make quite an incriminating picture. Calvin picked up the headphone flex and handed it to Mike. Mike let it fall again. The others had

alistair gentry

arrived, but warily kept their distance. Calvin didn't bother to count them, but they were numerous and obviously all out in the fields with purpose. The prevalence of motley jumble sale clothes, dreads, strategic shaving and various other manky hairstyles ruled out a Young Farmers' meeting. A dog started barking and pulling on the end of its rope. Its owner kept saying something to it, perhaps its name, but the dog ignored him.

'Didn't sound like nothing,' said a man who was dressed in black from his woollen hat right down to his vegan DMs. 'Are you alright, mate? I said are you alright, mate?'

Stereo Mike looked up at him and recoiled slightly, as if the man's face had done something unexpected and frightening. Mike's attention shifted to the dog. It continued to yap and strain. Mike closed his eyes and made three barely perceptible nods. I understand. The dog quietly lay down between its handler's boots, looking at him under its brows.

Calvin spotted some familiar orange worms; Scooter's hair. Underneath it, unsurprisingly, Scooter. Standing beside him was Leah, cleaning her glasses with the tail of her shirt and replacing them, as if she expected Calvin to be someone else when she could see properly.

monkey boys

'Are they something to do with you?' asked the man with the dog.

'Never saw him in my life,' said Leah, indicating Mike, who didn't seem to mind being talked about as if he wasn't there. He was now quite content, gazing down at some tractor marks baked into the soil.

'This is the brother I was telling you about,' Leah continued, 'Calvin, the one who works at MTI.'

A look ricocheted around the group. Seconds passed, one, two, three. Then a cataract of questions bore down upon his head.

LEAH INDICATED WHERE Calvin could slot his muscles in beside her, by the fire. It wasn't really what he would have called a camp, just a few tents and some sheets of plastic draped over branches. Leah said they'd probably have to leave after tomorrow. A couple of people kept getting plants from a big pile and throwing them, roots and all, into the fire. Sometimes the plants had seeds on them that popped and spat in the heat. Calvin also found himself sitting beside a man who appeared to be virtually catatonic. He looked like the kind of person who probably made a habit of pissing in small, enclosed public places. A medicinal cigarette burned unheeded in his trembling hand. Calvin jerked his head and rolled his eyes in the strange man's direction.

'Oh, that's Jeff,' said Leah. 'You alright, Jeff?'

Jeff got up and wandered away, like a distracted cow. Scooter and Leah laughed. A girl with dreadlocks gave Stereo Mike blankets, which he proceeded to mummify himself with.

'Poor sod though, really,' said Scooter, 'Apparently he went on hunger strike in the Eighties. They put him on life support even though his living will said not to. His daughter overruled it. Brain damage. Poor bastard.'

'Are you not worried about that kind of thing?' said Leah, 'Ending up in the state Jeff's in, or like that headphones bloke—'

'It's not been as bad as I thought. Weird, though,' Calvin said. 'It's like everything in the middle just goes. Everything that happens either makes you really happy or it seems so terrible you can't stand it.'

'Doesn't that get really boring?' Scooter asked.

'Yeah, well, most people live in a pretty boring world, don't they?'

Scooter shrugged, neither agreeing nor arguing.

'Injections, all the time. Look at my arm. Got more holes in me

monkey boys

than a teabag. The other thing is you have you have to watch what you're thinking, 'cause sometimes you can't help saying it.'

Leah snorted.

'Oh bloody hell, Calvin, that'd be really unusual for you wouldn't it?'

Calvin still wanted to know what they were all doing lurking in Millennium's fields, what his little sister had got herself into, and what the hell all this World 3K business was about.

'Short for World Three Thousand. We're here because the political system doesn't work. Nobody listens because we're saying things they don't want to hear. So we have to find other ways. Hit them where it really hurts. Right in the profits.'

The woman's name was Dee. What she'd just delivered was obviously a standard text. Her shirt bore a picture of the Queen, rendered in a lurid blue. On top of this were layers of what looked like men's clothes.

'We try to avoid violence, though. Well, Luke once attacked John Selwyn Gummer with a cattle prod, which I have to say I didn't necessarily disapprove of…'

Luke's pierced eyebrows raised disingenuously, but his mouth grinned.

'Steve nearly did time for setting fire to McKing Burger,' said Scooter. 'Nobody was hurt,' he added, after a look from Dee.

'Steve!' Calvin yelled, 'My man!'

A few other people applauded. Steve play-acted humility. Dee continued evenly, rising without effort above the din.

'Generally, we prefer to raise awareness. We've occupied a few places before now. A couple of months ago we issued a press release saying we'd got hold of a genetically engineered monkey from MTI.'

'Yeah,' said Luke, 'we had Anglia calling us up asking us about this body we said we'd found laying in a ditch.'

Dee laughed at the memory.

'It's a shame we didn't think of getting a dummy or something, actually making one for them so they could come and film it.'

'There are monkeys at the lab,' Calvin said. 'Nick said he saw their brains taken out and that.'

Dee turned to Steve and something passed silently between them.

'Do you remember that Christmas, there was a nativity scene in front of the church?' said Calvin, becoming excited, entering into the spirit of the things. Leah's expression indicated that he was

monkey boys

about to put her in an awkward place with her friends, but Calvin didn't notice.

'I had this car paint,' he continued, 'And I sprayed baby Jesus, Mary, all their faces black. Even the black one.'

If Leah had been a chameleon she would have disappeared herself into the night. The rest of them were looking at Calvin as if his friends all wore helmets and went on frequent day trips together.

'Was it some kind of political statement, is that what you're saying?' asked Dee, taking Calvin more seriously than he had expected.

'Nah, don't think so, it was just vandalism.'

Dee went off to help the others fetch more plants for burning. Calvin was just about able to wait until she was out of earshot.

'What does she look like?'

'I think she looks alright,' said Leah. 'If you're rude to her you fucking die.'

'Yeah, alright, but I mean you'd think twice about answering the door bell, wouldn't you?'

'She's a very brave woman. Worked at Millennium Therapeutics Irrational. A geneticist. She smuggled animals out for years before they even knew it was her. You see these plants? They're genetically engineered, modified, patented by MTI. They've got genes from animals, the animals they murder there, bacteria, genes from other plants. Nobody knows exactly, because they're all copyrighted and patented and secret. People are already eating all this stuff without knowing it. We've torn them all up and planted native trees.'

Leah flung a fistful of the offending plants onto the fire and, satisfied, watched the misshapes burn.

THE LAMBS IN THE NEXT FIELD lay motionless in sleep or vigilance. Nick overarmed the empty bottle towards them. He heard it land on the ground without smashing. The lambs were oblivious. Nick continued towards the source of the distant screams he'd heard a while ago.

In the little stand of trees was a bonfire, with people feeding it enthusiastically. It sunk in, slightly too late, that a ditch and a fence enclosed the wood. As Nick jumped there was a tearing pain. He landed on his knees, feeling the barbed wire twist in his

monkey boys

palm. A section of the fencing, more a matter of principal than a meaningful barrier, collapsed under Nick's drunken weight.

The air smelled of burned curry, Stereo Mike was nowhere in sight, and Nick began to wonder if he had made a terrible mistake. A woman who had been sitting on an old beer crate seemed to have delegated herself as the welcoming party.

'Are you drunk?' she demanded, approaching and folding her arms across layers that included an ABOLISH THE MONARCHY T-shirt, an unravelling granny-manufactured cardigan and a yellowish lumberjack shirt with room for the lumberjack as well as her.

'I am not drunk,' said Nick. 'Hardly at all. Charmed, by the way. Have you got a plaster?'

Dee looked like a social sciences lecturer who didn't take any shit, but was kind of likeable anyway. Even by the primitive light of the bonfire she seemed born to the overhead projector. She told him that he might as well come and join them since apparently there was an open house policy. When he had, she instructed Nick to listen carefully because she only ever did the roll call once. From left: Luke (victim of a berserk attack with a piercing gun, ethnic duffle coat), Leah (sitcom heroine after a disastrous crash

alistair gentry

diet), Calvin (that lump of mouth-breathing muscle, how did he get there? How long would it be before MTI noticed they were all missing?), Ian (profoundly lost first year physics student), Mongrel (children's telly presenter subjected to growth hormone treatment and gone feral), Emma (dreads, bomber jacket, combat trousers), Dave (dreads, absurd midsummer parka, combat trousers), Scooter (Seventies NHS glasses, orange hair), Space Monkey (head like a coconut and stick-on sidies, mother probably ate something she shouldn't have while pregnant), Martin (another crusty cliché, whippety Heinz 57 on a string who was also called Martin), Steve (old hand, hunt sab blacks and Balaclava rolled up into a hat), Other Steve (Escapee from Soviet Social Realist poster) and Jeff (the kind of wasted old hippie even the clichéd crusties hated). It surprised Nick to find that, without any particular exertion of will, he did remember. His prejudices and snap judgements acted as convenient mnemonics.

'Incredibly nice to meet you all and everything, but if you don't mind me asking, what the fuck are you doing here?'

'I was about to ask you something similar. What's going on over there tonight,' asked Dee semi-rhetorically, nodding towards where Nick supposed MTI was, 'is somebody filming a

monkey boys

remake of the Great Escape?'

A pile of clothes shrugged a blanket off its head, and Nick recognised Stereo Mike's headphones. There was a long scar on his neck that Nick had never noticed before. He asked Mike if he was OK. Mike nodded slowly, clearly a considerable distance from OK.

'We're all gonna get our pay docked, if they don't just kick us out on our arses.'

Again, Mike nodded, but this time he didn't stop. Nick's first impulse had been true. He should have simply gone back to bed and let the old vegetable roam the countryside in search of crusties, if that's what tripped his trigger.

'Yeah, we've already got two of yours,' muttered Steve. Dave came up behind him and yanked the Balaclava down over Steve's face. Steve took off in pursuit.

Dee shouted after them, obviously used to being the default mother. Dave and Steve were rolling around together in a patch of rhododendron as Steve tried to zip Dave's parka hood up into a tube.

'Children, please, I mean Jesus Christ. If you want to screw each other, just do it.'

alistair gentry

Dee disengaged herself, apparently satisfied that Nick was either far too hammered or not quite wasted enough to cause any trouble.

'Welcome to World Three Thousand,' she said over a departing shoulder.

'If you're looking for the pub, it's probably closed by now but it's about fifteen miles in the opposite direction,' grumbled Martin, who was doubtless an intercity dole scrounger. Little Martin, his mangy fleabag dog, scratched persistently inside its ear. Nick just looked at him.

'Well, if you don't like it, you know what you can do, don't ya? You can fuck off back to your lab,' Martin growled. Nick scrutinised the dog's whiskery face, incredulous. It continued to scratch vigorously.

'I only sign on in one place. I got a right to, whatever you might think. And there ain't no call for insulting a dog who ain't done you no harm.' Martin removed himself and his dog to sit under a filthy grey blanket with two head holes. Nick looked over at Calvin, who was examining his own biceps.

'Did I commit some kind of eco faux pas?'

'Mmm?'

monkey boys

'What did I do to offend him?'

'Well, saying he was a scrounger and that. I mean, he might be, but—'

Calvin turned away to see what Leah and Scooter were up to. They weren't doing anything, not even talking, just sitting and looking into the flames in the way that people tend to do.

'Did I really say that?'

Nick needed a piss. The stuff they were giving him was too weird. He didn't like it. It was only being tanked up that was keeping him sane.

'Wait a minute. What about that, did I say that out loud too?'

Calvin's attention swung back again. He looked about eleven, as if he had just been caught shoplifting by his mum.

'What did I say just then, if anything?' asked Nick.

'Something about being tanked up?' Calvin replied, his mind obviously elsewhere. Nick went off to relieve himself, satisfied that he was as much in control of his faculties as he ever was.

After sitting by the fire Nick felt convinced the temperature away from it was hovering around freezing, but apparently it was more like Ibiza if you had a donkey jacket and the inclination. When he complained, Steve gave him a withering look. Nick left it at that. You're alright, gorilla features, you've got a coat and a Balaclava. Nick found himself spending about a fiver. Such a little body and so much urine. He couldn't seem to stop himself looking at Steve's dick as they pissed into the ditch. Steve retaliated by checking out Nick's. It being cold and dark, all things were relatively equal. As Nick tottered away, he pointed at the number seven on the front of his shirt, intending to indicate marks out of ten. Steve didn't seem to understand, just zipped himself up and shook his head.

Nick headed back towards the fire, but suddenly felt too hot so he sat down more or less where he was, against a trunk. After a while Emma came along and leaned against the warmer side of the tree. Nick hoped that she was about to do him a favour and ask him to examine her body piercings. She knew he was irresistible, didn't she? He was still horny. Emma started going on about direct action, occupation of the labs, other stuff. It was all very interesting, but not to Nick, unfortunately. Mental age higher than five please, Nick thought, and went off her a bit. It didn't stop him trying it on.

'Don't touch me,' Emma informed him, 'doesn't mean wait, then touch me.'

monkey boys

When he persisted and tried to explain that he was doing a drug study, he wasn't normally like this, she offered him a punch in the face. In lieu of that, Nick agreed that they should part amicably. He moved closer to the fire again.

Close up, Dee was actually quite stylish in an unusual, got dressed in the dark kind of way. Unlike Emi, Nick couldn't imagine Dee having more underwear than any woman in the Western World, or objecting to a grown man eating cereal at seven in the evening. Temperamental, dreadlocked Emma managed to menace without Nick even being able to see her properly (how did she do that?). Mike was still where Nick left him, safely bundled in his own thoughts. Dee made no attempt to shift up on her beer crate, so Nick sat beside her and staked his claim by leaning an elbow on it.

'Sorry if I said anything out of order earlier,' he mumbled, trying to pitch his voice so that only Dee would hear.

'I suppose it's OK,' she said vaguely, without looking up from the stuff she was eating from an icecream tub. It smelled of curry but looked like baby food.

'It's just I find it hard to believe that by living in a shoebox and not washing your hair you're going to make the world a better place.'

'I thought you were apologising?' Dee looked down at him. 'Anyway, I have to say I find it amazing that such a big head can have such a small, narrow mind inside it.'

'Don't you ever feel guilty for being so complacent and comfortable?' said Other Steve, through a roll up. Nick shrugged.

'I can afford to be complacent because I *am* comfortable.'

Dee swallowed another mouthful of the yellowish mush from her tub.

'You see?' she said, 'Everyone can smell cynicism on you like cigarette smoke.'

'I suppose you don't smoke, either?'

'Not since my husband died of lung cancer, no,' she replied, unemotional, and dug into her tub. Seeing that curry disappear between her teeth without pause for emotion or effect, Nick respected her and her beliefs more than he had. There was obviously more to Dee than she usually cared to show, and perhaps the same was true of the others. They were so wrong that they were almost right. Nearly everyone Nick knew, and Nick himself, nursed vague fantasies about escaping the routines they had trapped themselves in, and trying to create lives that made at least a little bit more sense. That was the deal. Other Steve threw

monkey boys

the ciggie he'd just lit into the fire.

'They've known smoking gives people cancer since the Fifties,' Steve blurted suddenly, as if someone had pushed a button.

Emma was listening, too.

'Then they sell us bogus cures for the diseases they've given us.'

'Look,' said Nick, edging forward and talking with his hands, 'I'm not actually disagreeing with you, but all this conspiracy stuff doesn't make any sense. There are bastards that need nailing, I'm not denying it, but talking like that just lets them dismiss you as naive or stupid. Nobody's conspiring against us. The stupidity, selfishness and greed of most people on the planet is the only conspiracy.'

Possibly Nick wasn't deluding himself when he thought that Dee was looking at him with new appreciation after this unusually articulate outburst.

'You're right,' she said, finally placing that damn tub on the soil, 'The things people are afraid of now are just their old complacencies, exaggerated, but that can change. It can change.'

'Things don't have to be the way they are,' agreed Other Steve, one step away from leaping up and shouting hallelujah.

'You see, I wish I had your faith,' said Nick, hands chopping and grasping at the muggy air again. 'I'm desperate for something to change, too. No, I'm not, actually. I'm desperate for nothing in particular for no particular reason. At least you're sincere.'

'I hate that word,' Dee said sharply. 'Sincere is absolutely poisonous. I don't think any of us would ever sit here congratulating ourselves on how sincere we are. At least, I hope not. Christ.'

'What I want is to know what I'm supposed to do in the world,' said Nick, his voice shrinking, almost pleading. 'I want that instinct for how things work. Not to keep thinking about what I should have done, but didn't because I was too busy thinking about the past…'

Dee was peering up through the heat wilted leaves, trying to see the sky.

'It's going to rain,' she said. She was obviously covering a delay in her thought processes with these weather words, because immediately afterwards she turned to Nick and said, with a fervent look and the light of the fire in her eyes,

'What you want is for someone to save you.'

He shrugged. 'I'm not aware of wanting to be saved. Yes, I am. No, I'm not,' and he couldn't help laughing at himself. 'Don't psychoanalyse me.'

monkey boys

There was a pressure in the air, not unpleasant, as if Dee was correct and it really was about to rain. He couldn't see where her eyes had wandered this time.

'Do you steal the condiment packets from cafés and hoard them so you won't have to buy any?' said Nick, trying to get her back. He thought she had stopped listening.

'Yeah,' she replied after a while. 'I knew I couldn't be the only one.'

Nick scrutinised Dee by pretending to look past her at Calvin and Leah's dwindling figures. They meandered back towards the labs, trampling yet another line through that unnatural wheat; he with his eight still on inside out, carrying a camera and a big aluminium case, she swinging an enormous pair of bolt cutters, a loop of cable over one shoulder. Nick imagined their paths spelling out a message for tomorrow's sky and hoped they'd be lucky.

Stereo Mike wished there was a newspaper or a TV station he could phone to inform the world of his decision to commit suicide. They could despatch a crew to document the event.

It seemed a waste that something so edifying should have such a small audience. The ideal outcome would be for the telly people to get his mother down here and have her apologise nationwide for the way she'd treated him. For the things she let his father do to him. Blame her, blame him, blame everything, anything. After hearing his mother's apology, he would say what he had always intended to:

WELL IT'S STILL YOUR FAULT BITCH.

Then fall into the flames.

That's where he was. In the flames, looking out through a cage of agony and fire. It was him, the smoke of himself, that was burning in Mike's nose and throat. He used to wonder why the stunt men on television always flailed about like they did. Now he knew, blinded, choked and numb with pain, his body's instincts pugilistic. He did not want to die. Mike could not ignore his body's talent for survival any more. He had been a victim so often because he was good at it. No more. What he needed now was help, not a light.

Dee, Nick and the protesters gazed on, hardly seeming to blink, as if it was a soap they wanted to see conclude but knew would be picked up season after season.

monkey boys

The metal in Luke's face caught Mike's light and glinted.

Then Nick was attacking Mike with blankets, followed by Dee and Scooter, as if they detected Mike's psychic distress flare, smothering the death that crawled all over his body but finally had to give him up one more time.

N**ICK THOUGHT** Stereo Mike looked more sunburned than anything, although one of his hands was pretty bad. All things considered, he didn't look much worse than Nick had after he tried to light a cigarette from the bonfire without taking it out of his mouth first.

Nick studied Mike for a long time, trying to work out why he looked even stranger than before. It dawned on him eventually that Mike's eyebrows had burned off. His ponytail was gone, too, so his hair hung in irregular, frazzled strands around his face. His stupid fringe now looked ridiculously stylish. People came up and put their arms around Mike, their hands on Nick's arm. Nick cried, they cried, but Mike just stared out into the fields as if he was waiting for a taxi to come and pick him up. The LCD of his watch was totally black.

'It wasn't brave,' Nick demurred. 'He had my cigarettes in his pocket.'

It rained.

MIKE UNDERMINED HIS FAITH in his own memories with drugs. He looked back on his life and he was remembering things, but he didn't know whether he trusted his brain enough to believe anything it told him.

Everything became suspect, including the story Mike had constructed of himself. The aliens weren't coming. He'd been fooled. All context had gone. No, everything in the context of what happened after, what was happening now. All conflated and collated from different seasons and times or moments. Things that possibly weren't real, all the things his mother said and all the things she never did, all the ellipses.

Mike did almost remember some data about himself that was very close to true. Not in any visceral way. Not because he thought he should. It was more like something frightening he had

monkey boys

once watched on the telly and then tried to go to sleep on.

The rain gave no indication of ever stopping. A boy and a girl were out in the field, dancing in it. Mike never learned to swim because of a bad experience with his father in the bath when he was four. His dad couldn't swim either. Eventually his dad jumped off the end of Southend Pier to get over a fear of water that was both rational and stupid. Obliterated himself and his secrets before he was caught. The only sensible idea anyone in Mike's family ever had.

When Mike finally began to speak, he couldn't stop again. He told the man in the seven about everything that had ever been in his world. As they sat under the plastic, Stereo Mike seemed to be doing all the talking but it didn't matter. His voice went on a long time after he had said everything there was to say. That's all Mike was, just a voice inside a drum that the rain played endlessly.

His eyes filled with tears while he was speaking, as if the water was pouring into them as well as onto the plastic. Mike stood, turned away from the numbered man who had comforted him with silence, hugged himself tightly. There was an endless moment with nothing in it except rain. The wind, blowing hard and steady from the East, idly flipped something metallic and

alistair gentry

close as dawn collapsed on top of them like a paralytic stranger and finally everyone slept.

CALVIN'S BARCODED WRIST BAND got them as far as a corridor adjoining one of Monkey Island's laboratories. He suspected the two of them were setting off alarms in every doorway and staircase, even if they weren't audible. At first Leah tried smashing the card reader with her bolt cutters. When this didn't work, she swung them at the safety glass in the door. She was surprisingly handy with a pair of industrial bolt cutters. With a third blow the glass grudgingly gave inwards. They were officially breaking. Leah made Calvin cram himself through the hole first, so he could get a good shot of her doing the entering part. The smell in there made Calvin want to puke, but he did as Leah instructed; put his eye to the camera.

Along one side of the room most of the monkeys managed some ragged sleep. A few insomniacs sat staring through the mesh, past the walls, to the horizon. Their colleagues opposite were obviously tripping out of their nuts; hiding in terror or poking

monkey boys

and grasping at illusory objects. Sharp little smiles of panic, tails that flickered from question mark to exclamation mark and back again. Leah hit the lights and their scrawny, sad bodies cowered away from the fluorescence. Some of the monkeys had arms and legs so perforated by jabbing needles they were just masses of swollen hairy pink flesh and dirty scabs. The silent ones were worse, slack faces babbling silently about brain damage.

In the fridge Calvin and Leah found ampoules of experimental drugs, blood samples, Diet Cokes and a neatly severed monkey head in a plastic bag. It wore a strangely gratified expression. Look at me, it seemed to say. They had to saw my damn head off to beat me.

Ten cages stood apart from the others. All but one, A55 HL, was empty. It was impossible to tell if the inmate was sleeping. Its eyelids were brutally sutured, closing them forever. Leah opened the cage before Calvin could stop her. She told him to shut up and film, just film. As its prison swung open, the monkey flung up miniature hands to push against new barriers the product was constructing from the brain's restricted input. One skeletal wrist wore a disproportionately huge tag, similar to Calvin's. Leah's eyes couldn't help themselves as she grasped the skinny baby,

alistair gentry

gently persuaded the frightened arms to rest. She wet a thumb to rub at the monkey's forehead, where someone had biroed letters. Even this small kindness provoked a fit of imaginary insects. So, the monkey had to remain ARSEHOLE.

The infant took refuge in Leah's elbow, burying its face, instinctively hiding from a world it had never seen. Leah worked fingers under her glasses to wipe away the tears that wouldn't stop. Rendered rectangular on the camera's tiny screen, the image reminded Calvin vaguely of something. What it was, or where it came from, he didn't know. It was nothing to do with Leah, but Calvin was jealous. He knew his tribulations were nothing compared to some, but a blind monkey had achieved what Calvin always wanted. He'd never been able to tell anyone, ask doesn't get. Just to be held, that's all it was. Just to be held in arms that loved him.

It was about then that the alarms, long overdue, started to sing like hungry chicks with megaphones.

monkey boys

Nick is wearing one of his dad's sports jackets and a clip-on tie. He darts from bush to car to tree as he imagines James Bond would, if he ever found himself on a quiet street in Essex. Climbing on somebody's car with Scott and Johnny, all of them wearing his mum's high heels, for reasons now erased forever. Nick gets a stuffed toy monkey for his birthday every year. He doesn't often give them names. He usually burns them in November.

The next day came like a punch in the face. Nick kept his lids firmly closed, his eyes still scanning furiously for images he knew he would never retrieve, redream or remember now. He hated waking up with a hangover and not being able to brush his teeth. His sleep had been long but not profound.

The barbed wire fence was a clothesline for windblown plastic bags. What Nick had interpreted as lambs the night before were actually huge blocks of polystyrene packing. He supposed it was probably the wrong time of year for lambs anyway.

The corn and grass outside the fence were allegedly organic, but looked like they were made of acrylic. The rape was Dulux Summer Rape. Nick assumed it was what other people would call red. From the wood, MTI's jumble of buildings looked like the Twentieth century had chucked out its rubbish. It was making distant noises, but even these couldn't intrude. Unseen beyond it was the wilderness of Judo, the place that used to dump him on his arse with such monotonous regularity. He didn't think it would throw him so often in future, because he wouldn't let it use his own weight against him. Nick enjoyed the loneliness for a moment, allowed it to seep into his ears and through his skin.

Eventually he couldn't ignore the bustle of the rapidly disappearing camp any longer. They said Luke had gone early to the hospital, with Stereo Mike on the back of his bicycle. Ian, the kid who looked like he'd got lost on his way to a lecture, was more credible in daylight with a phone propped against his shoulder. He was pacing around, grasping ziplock bags full of MTI's property, the modified plants Nick saw burning.

'The original bacterium is only poisonous in the digestive systems of the caterpillars who naturally feed on the leaves. The engineered versions secrete an active form of the toxin throughout the plant's life cycle. Well, no, it's very bad...'

Dee looked how Nick felt: tired out and irrationally jubilant. He wondered what her excuse was. She was carrying a boring

monkey boys

grey box with interesting trailing cables that disappeared into her collection of pockets.

'I was up all night with the laptop,' she said, without Nick needing to comment.

'Lucky laptop,' Nick replied, trying not to smoke in her direction.

Dee let him have that one. Without a word she unfolded the computer so Nick could see what was on the screen: a pixellated, frozen moment of motion.

Steve was sufficiently fired up to have discarded his hunt sab blacks for a crumpled T-shirt, its front overpopulated by the assertion that GENETIC ENGINEERING IS A JUMBO JET WITH BICYCLE BRAKES. Calvin and his sister were still barricaded inside the monkey laboratory, and had been broadcasting all night. Nick conceded to himself that you had to love a shithead like that. A man who threw himself into everything, *everything*, unhindered by realism or experience, untainted by common sense. Everyone watched in silent delight as the police, media and PR vehicles crawled anxiously along the narrow road to MTI. Dee looked into Nick's eyes for a long time.

They were too late, no matter who they arrested, soundbit or

alistair gentry

lied to. The information was already free. Nick finally deciphered what he was looking at on the computer. A framegrab of a distraught young monkey, moving left out of frame, eyes sewn shut, ARSEHOLE inscribed on its forehead. A barcoded wrist tag, identical to the one Nick was still wearing, unquestionably bore the MTI logo. Nick had to sit down against a tree.

He rested his eyes until Dee came along and drove her boot into his hand as forcefully as she could. Before he finished screaming she tore off last night's plaster. Dee swabbed the blood and delivered it into a series of the ubiquitous ziplock bags that, like the laptop's wires, vanished into her pockets. She apologised. It didn't sound very sincere, but Nick was prepared to believe she was sorry.

'It was your eyes,' she said. 'The drug obviously persists in the body for at least twenty-four hours. With samples we can get it analysed, publish the chemical composition—'

Perhaps the product was still working on him. As Nick looked at his bleeding hand, the lines in his palm seemed freighted with a significance that fluttered just beyond his grasp.

'What would that achieve?'

'Oh, not much. But it'd get right up their noses.'

monkey boys

Dee shrugged and produced another plaster, which hardly seemed up to the task of repairing his crushed hand.

'Or,' she said, with equal emphasis, 'you can just go crawling back to Millennium and try to get what they owe you. Sell out while you've still got the chance.'

Nick wasn't sure whether or not he had an idea to take home after all the excitement was over, when the excitement had only just begun. It might just have been that there could be a whole new breed of mutants, anxious to exist. Or perhaps it was that the world sometimes caved in at a second's notice, so he might as well accept the only two alternatives that made any sense. He could start living or he could keep on dying.

'I think a morning like this calls for grand, futile gestures,' he said.

Nick made it through (the) Millennium to die of something much more interesting and futuristic in the next one. Things never got back under any kind of control. Having control had gone out of the window, along with so many other things. Nick didn't feel as if he was fighting the future any more. The only thing he knew was that it was ahead of him. It was just…there, always rising to meet him and falling back again like surf. Stereo Mike and Calvin

alistair gentry

and Dee and Leah and Scooter and Nick in it, being not as young as they were, doing their best, trying not to fear the worst.

It was an incandescent Tuesday that smelled of whatever they had sprayed on the fields and evaporating rain, one summer late in the century. Nick felt as though something had come to an end, even if he had no idea what it was. The pouring sun stung his eyes, almost blinded him because his pupils were still the size of 10ps. Not newly minted ones either, but those giant bastards from the Seventies. He was walking and falling at the same time, not looking for anything or anyone. Stepping out into the blue room. Making a random start. It was morning, there was a hole in the fence and if there hadn't been, Nick would happily have cut his hands again to climb it.

His memories hurt.

He took them out into the fields and ploughed them under.

END

Praise for Alistair Gentry's first novel:

A smart, accomplished and sharply focused satire / **i-D**

Full of bizarre and fresh ideas, Alistair Gentry weaves together a surreal and outrageously inventive story. Right up my street / **Scotland on Sunday**

A writer to watch out for / **Evening Standard**

A bilious critique of haywire consumerism and corporate hypocrisy, 'Their Heads are Anonymous' succeeds in being simultaneously repulsive, engrossing and hilarious. Book of the month / **G-Spot**

This saucy, breezy and cool satire on theme park McJobbery also features psychic insects / **D-Tour**

Resolutely subversive / **SFX**

Alistair Gentry was born in 1973. He lives in a windswept, forgotten British seaside resort where he claims never to have had a proper job, although in a weak moment he owned up to once having worked in an internet cafe. In 1997 Pulp Books published his well received first novel, 'Their Heads Are Anonymous'. Several of Gentry's plays have been produced, and he won a Write Out Loud award in 1999. Alistair Gentry is a dedicated non-Londoner.